Library of Congress Cataloging-in-Publication Data is available.

ISBN (10): 1-59376-231-3
ISBN (13): 978-1-59376-231-5

Cover design by Shane Luitjens
Printed in the United States of America

Soft Skull Press
An Imprint of Counterpoint LLC
2117 Fourth Street
Suite D
Berkeley, CA 94710

www.softskull.com
www.counterpointpress.com

Distributed by Publishers Group West

10 9 8 7 6 5 4 3 2 1

Lux the Poet

Martin Millar

SOFT SKULL PRESS

BROOKLYN

Lying with a Friend under a Burnt-out Truck

Lying under the burnt-out truck, head still bleeding and cocaine still rampaging around his body, Lux the Poet begins to ramble.

"I have definitely had a hard life you know. When I was nine I fell under a lawnmower. It was an experimental model my dad was testing for the company. It could've been a disaster. It could've cut my head off. Worse, it could've left me so horribly scarred I'd've been ashamed to walk the streets. All it did though was give me this nice little scar over my eye which as you can see makes me even more attractive. This is why I'm permanently optimistic. Even a terrible lawnmower accident turned out well."

His companion listens in silence.

"In fact," continues Lux, megalomaniac vanity coming to the surface, I am universally acknowledged to be the prettiest man on the planet. Also I'm the greatest poet. Despite this I am unappreciated. I always suspected my dad deliberately shoved me under the lawnmower. He hated me because I was a test tube baby. It is not widely known but I am the first test tube baby to become a nationally recognised poet."

"You're not nationally recognised."

"It's only a matter of time. I wrote my first great poem when I was seven. An epic."

"What was it about?"

"Oral sex with a shark. It created a sensation. I got expelled from my primary school. They said I'd disgraced them in the road safety contest. Apparently it was the only sex-with-a-shark poem in the under-nine category. But it worked out well enough. Everyone at my next primary school wanted to hear my poetry. And ever since then I've been thrilling the nation. Do you want to hear a poem?"

"Not right now Lux."

"Why not?"

"Because we're lying under a burnt-out truck in a riot."

Lux can't follow this, it seems to him like the ideal time. Nevermind.

"Is my hair still perfect?"

"Shut up Lux."

1

AT SEVENTEEN, Lux the Poet is a natural optimist, undeterred by life's misfortunes.

Being hopelessly in love with a girl called Pearl who doesn't care for him all that much could count as a misfortune, but Lux always imagines that people he likes enough are bound to like him back sooner or later and in view of the wonderful new poem he has written for her it will probably be sooner.

He thinks about her all the time, and supposes that she thinks of him.

Pearl is at this moment trying to shepherd her friend Nicky through a riot. Nicky is practically comatose with worry, the shops in the main street of Brixton are starting to burn, it is becoming hard to hear over the sound of shouts and sirens and breaking glass, hard to move in the crowds that are alternately advancing in triumph or retreating in disarray, and generally no fun at all for someone intent only on finding some safety.

So right now Pearl is not spending much time thinking about Lux.

"I killed my computer. Don't let them artificially inseminate me," moans Nicky obscurely, and Pearl drags her on.

The misfortunes that Lux is not too worried about include having nowhere to live and no Giros coming from the social security but he figures it will work out all right in the end.

He strides through the riot, not too worried about it, on his way to Pearl's house. "Hello," he says, passing by someone he knows who is busy throwing rocks at the police across the street.

He gets a nod in return.

Lux is friendly to most people, and polite.

Passing by the corner of a small street he ducks his head down, not wanting to be spotted by the woman who lives on the top floor, an ex-lover who on learning that as well as sleeping with her and eating her food he was also going to bed with her sister, her brother, and two of her friends tried to throw him out of the window. A total over-reaction as far as Lux could see, but not an experience he wants to repeat. He is just not strong enough to fight off irate lovers.

Due to his devastating good looks, the area is full of men and women who want to fuck him although they wouldn't necessarily want him to stay around and talk about it afterwards because Lux has a terrible habit of trying to make people listen to his poetry.

"I don't want to go down to Brixton just now," protests Mark, listening to the news on the radio. "There is a riot going on."

"So what?" Gerry is entirely dismissive of the objection. "If there is a riot on then that is where we should be. The people need our support. Besides, we have to get the manuscript back."

When Lux arrives at Pearl's house he finds it burned to the ground.

Tears well up in his eyes. As a young artist he can cope with almost any aspect of a tragic love affair but not his girlfriend being burned to death.

"Little poppies, little hell flames," mutters Lux, a fan of Sylvia Plath.

"Pearl is all right," a neighbour tells him, bringing out a cup of tea for a sweating fireman. "She went off with a friend."

Well that's a relief, thinks Lux. I couldn't have coped with an incinerated Pearl. And now she needs me more than ever. He sets off in pursuit.

A shame it had to happen before he arrived. Possibly he might have been able to fight his way into the burning building and rescue her and been a hero.

Lux has no idea what the riot is about. It just sort of started while he was walking along the street. When he first saw a gang of youths running towards him he thought perhaps it was some fans come to hear some poetry and was disappointed when they ran on past without paying him any attention.

This feeling persists, however, and the whole night Lux has a subconscious suspicion that possibly the riot is in his honour.

The riot, grumbling away from the early afternoon, heats up as the evening comes.

Pearl had the misfortune to have her house burned down very early on, before things were even really under way. A stray petrol bomb bounced off a policeman's riot shield, shattered her window, and set alight the curtains. Modern technology has made riot shields very efficient, which is good for the policemen but bad for anyone else around when petrol bombs get thrown.

Old and threadbare, the curtains blazed up in seconds and that was that. Pearl barely had time to grab a few possessions, including her valuable film, and flee, dragging along her friend Nicky, currently hiding from Happy Science PLC and going through a massive trauma over what she did to her computer.

So now she is trying to work her way through Brixton to Kennington where she can find refuge with a friend for her and Nicky and her film, but with the police blocking off roads everywhere to isolate the riot it is very hard going.

Lux was evicted from his squat five days ago. This took him by surprise because he hadn't bothered to look at any of the official letters of eviction he had been sent so all he had time to gather up was a few clothes and some prized possessions like his Star Wars toothbrush and picture of Lana Turner, whom he resembles. He didn't have all that much stuff anyway, but it did mean leaving behind his collection of brightly coloured carrier bags and some poetry books he'd stolen here and there, and also his dungarees. As he is commonly acknowledged to look sensational in dungarees, this is a sad loss.

So now he has no proper place to live and has been staying with Mike and Patrick, who don't mind him moving in for a while so long as he doesn't try to read them any of his poems.

This is difficult for Lux to do, as he likes reading his poems to people, in fact he loves it, but he controls the urge as best he can because as well as giving him a roof over his head they have been feeding him and this is not something to be laughed at, especially when the DHSS is saying that he has to make his benefit claim all over again because he didn't tell them about his change of address, and a new benefit claim takes long enough for a person to starve.

However, his habit of borrowing or stealing anything not too heavy for him to carry and then shamelessly lying about it afterwards has been causing some tension in the household.

Nicky is unfortunately being no help to Pearl because she is virtually in a coma having suffered severe shock when she destroyed her computer at work. Her computer was her only friend apart from Pearl and now she regards herself as a murderer. Furthermore she is convinced that Happy Science are after her and it is all too much for her mind to take so it has started to switch off intermittently and she is liable at any time to wander off into a looting mob or a police Transit van without realising what she is doing. So Pearl has to coax her along and the going is becoming increasingly difficult as more and more people flood out onto the streets with wild smiles and petrol bombs and more buildings start to burn.

The riot begins in the young black community and spreads to the whites and they join forces to fight the police.

Cars trying to pass through Brixton are stopped and the occupants robbed and their vehicles set on fire so the police try to prevent any more vehicles coming in by setting up roadblocks but with frightened drivers going all ways and everything and everyone a mass of excitement, terror and confusion the streets are soon impassably blocked with burning and abandoned heaps of scrap metal, some overturned like horrible giant beetles, some sitting quietly with their tyres smouldering, and all with their doors and windows open to the world—in-car-radioless, stereo-speakerless, tyreless, never-to-be-traded-in, valueless hulks.

The sky rains with stones and any other missile that comes to hand and the police, reinforcements arriving in their special green buses, start forming up with their shields and batons to make advances towards the rioters and Pearl, caught in the middle with a sick friend and a film to look after, becomes more and more worried.

Like Lux, she can cope with another riot, but this time she has things to protect.

Kalia, exile from Heaven, goes through reincarnation after reincarnation doing kindness after kindness. She has to.

Exiled from Heaven after being framed in a celestial coup that went wrong, Kalia is dragged in front of the Heavenly Court where she is sentenced to perform five hundred thousand acts of kindness before being re-admitted into Heaven. She will have to eternally reincarnate until she has worked off the badness of being involved in a coup against the Gods.

"But I never did anything," she protests. "I was framed."

"Silence," roars her judge." You spend your time writing subversive poetry. You were obviously involved. For talking back you are now sentenced to do a million good deeds. Now go."

The next thing she knows she is waking up as a newly born child in a poverty-stricken peasant community on the southern tip of India.

After the splendours of Heaven it is a terrible comedown. A million acts of kindness. How long is that going to take?

"If we go down to Brixton we might get attacked," says Mark, worried.

"Attacked?" Gerry looks at him with disgust. "Why would we get attacked? The riot is against police and oppressison. I am not the police or an oppressor, am I? Why would I be attacked?"

Mark gazes at Gerry admiringly. He is so smart. He writes for *Uptown*, a left-wing arts magazine. There is nothing he doesn't know.

"As soon as I finish this writing we'll catch the tube," he says.

2

Lux is not too worried about the riot because it is the third one he has lived through and he never came to harm in either of the others.

He is slightly perturbed however to find Pearl's house burned down. Neither of the previous riots has had any effect on him but this could have been a tragedy.

He tramps the streets looking for her, knowing that he can be of assistance, knowing that he will be a star one day, muttering snatches of other people's poetry, making up his own.

A white van pulls up beside him and Lux is interested to see a camera crew emerge. He would like to be on television.

"Hello," he says politely as they set up their cameras. "I am Lux, an important local poet. Would you like to hear one of my poems?"

"No," says the reporter. He is busy looking round for a hot story and local poets are rarely hot stories. Lux is a little disappointed, although he is used to people not wanting to hear his poems. He appreciates that there is little taste for the truly artistic in the world any more.

The camera starts filming the riot. Lux, however, guardian of artistic sensibilities, is not so easy to get rid of and starts working his way in front of it.

"Are you sure you wouldn't like to hear a poem?"

"Absolutely."
"Why not?"
"I'm busy."
"Doing what?"
"Will you get the hell out of here! We're trying to film a riot."

Lux starts declaiming a poem anyway, figuring it is more interesting than a riot, but the soundman, used to outsiders trying to muscle in on the act, works the controls so that no one can hear him and Lux declaims his poem into the void.

The people that Lux is living with, Patrick and Mike, live far up Brixton Hill and are so far unaffected by the riot. They are watching it on the news.

"Another riot," says Patrick. "Oh God, there's Lux trying to get in front of a camera again."

Mike laughs but Patrick sniffs with disapproval. He does not really want Lux in the house and only puts up with it because Mike likes him, and as he thinks that the reason Mike likes Lux is that he wants to fuck him he does not really approve at all. It makes him jealous.

They watch as the camera swings back and forward trying to focus on rioters while Lux determinedly pursues the lens to keep himself in the picture, all the while mouthing off something that nobody can hear.

Happy Science is in turmoil. Their well-publicised research project to breed a new generation of geniuses is in big trouble.

The project involves a vastly complicated genetic programme and gathering of semen from old geniuses and implanting it into suitable women.

They plan to breed a very clever new generation.

The prime minister is thrilled with the idea. It has caught the public imagination, partly because they are also running a beauty contest to decide on some suitable mothers.

It was originally planned to find some genius mothers as well, but the Happy Science publicity department vetoed the idea, feeling that they would get more attention from the press with some beauty queens.

Unfortunately the genetic programme has gone missing and without the genetic programme all they have is a few test tubes full of frozen sperm.

Doctor Carlson, head of the project, buries his face in his hands. Disaster is looming on every front. His Nobel Prize hangs in the balance. He should never have tried to blackmail Nicky into entering the beauty contest.

Lux is easily recognisable on the TV screen, looking something like a cross between a scarecrow and Lana Turner, if Lana Turner had red and yellow hair standing in a jagged bush two feet off her head and the scarecrow topped its ragged old coat with a face of extreme girlish beauty, bearing a little piratical scar over its left eye.

Lux is regarded by some people, particularly himself, as the prettiest man in London, if not the whole world.

Patrick thinks he is a little brat.

"Little brat," says Patrick.

"Leave him alone," replies Mike. "I like him."

"And we all know why."

"Whadya mean we all know why?"

"You know what I mean we all know why."

"No I don't know what you mean . . ."

This goes on for a while.

"You're in a bad mood because Liberation Computers is losing money again."

"That's not true!"

Mike is very sensitive about Liberation Computers, a business he has set up with his friend Marcus using the social security set-up-your-own-business scheme for reducing the unemployment figures. They start to argue about the washing up.

Recently their relationship has not been running very smoothly and were it not for the fact that their sex life is very good they might well have broken up some time ago.

OK, thinks Lux, walking away from the TV crew. So you don't want to hear my poems. Fine. Fuck you. You wouldn't know a good poet if he bit you in the leg.

But it is a little dispiriting, the way no one ever wants to listen to him. Everyone just automatically assumes that what he has to say is nonsense.

"It is prejudice," he mutters. "They won't listen to my poems because I have perfect legs like Betty Grable. If Shakespeare had had legs like Betty Grable he wouldn't have stood a chance either."

He catches sight of himself in a flame-illuminated shop window and this cheers him up, as always. It is a good thing, he thinks, that I am so attractive. I would have found it hard to cope with life if I wasn't. I wonder how everyone else manages?

Having given up the attempt to read the camera crew some poems, Lux has resumed his search.

Pearl cannot be all that far away, he reasons, particularly if she is with Nicky. Nicky is no doubt being difficult. She is practically in a coma these days.

Lux is not all that fond of Nicky. He suspects that she is sleeping with Pearl and that this is why Pearl has so far refused to fall in love with him. They have fucked several times but Lux knows that Pearl's heart was not in it. Lux can fuck all day long if he wants. He has many admirers. But he is desperate for Pearl to fall in love with him.

Momentarily a feeling that life is very hard descends upon him. Here he is, monumentally good looking and the most talented writer the world has ever seen and still Pearl doesn't seem to be particularly attracted to him. He can't understand it.

When he sends his work off to magazines they never say nice things about it. Yes, he muses, it is a solitary life, guarding the artistic heritage of the nation. He bumps into some people he knows, hurrying home away from the riot.

"Have you seen Pearl?" he asks.

"Pearl who?"

"Just Pearl," he says, realising that he doesn't know her surname. He wonders if she has one. Presumably.

Seeing no alternative, the Gods being too powerful to fight against, Kalia sets about her million acts of kindness. Almost as soon as she can walk she is carrying water for the women of the village and helping chop firewood for the family and volunteering for extra skinning duties on the odd occasions that the hunters bring in a deer or a gazelle.

"That child is a saint," says her mother to a friend.

"Only another nine hundred and ninety nine thousand, nine hundred and eighty two to go, sighs the young Kalia, sadly, already finding it difficult.

Johnny is an important man these days in Personal Computer Services, otherwise known as the computer police. He is now engaged on a mission to track down Nicky who has committed the terrible crime of destroying a computer at Happy Science. You can't do this sort of thing to a big company and get away with it.

Lux stops everyone he knows and some people he doesn't and asks them if they have seen Pearl but nobody has. He asks people if they will help him look but everybody is too busy rioting.

At the offices of *Uptown* magazine Gerry is rushing through his work so he can get down to Brixton and report on the riot. He is editing the letters page.

You dumb bastard, he writes in response to a complaint from some fool who has gone to see a film he recommended and found it dull. I said it was a good film and I meant it. No doubt you were too busy eyeing up the woman in the next row to pay attention properly. Don't whine to us about wasting a valuable portion of your Giro and then not liking the film, we can't help it if you have the taste of a warthog.

As well as not being appreciated as a literary genius, Lux has to sleep on a couch at Mike and Patrick's and it is not a very nice couch. It is the sort of couch that is dragged by its owner from squat to squat before ending up in the front room of a hard-to-let council flat covered by an old blanket in a futile attempt to hide the beer and cigarette stains and it is really not all that pleasant to sleep on.

Lux, however, veteran of a score of temporary unfurnished squats and never much good at getting hold of any furniture, has rarely had anything very pleasant to sleep on unless someone with a proper home takes him in for the night so he wouldn't mind the discomfort too much except that downstairs live all the members of the Jane Austen Mercenaries, a local thrash metal band who he hates because he keeps having to listen to their demo tape through the floor. Thrash metal offends his artistic sensitivities at the best of times and listening to a four-song demo tape a hundred times a night really makes him feel that the band should be tied up in a sack and drowned, although he has never actually said this to them as sometimes they give him free cocaine.

Bricks and bottles fly overhead but Lux takes no notice, too intent on scanning the streets for a sign of Pearl.

"Was Milton ever evicted from his squat?" he mutters. "Did Thomas Hardy have to listen constantly to a thrash metal demo tape? No chance. These people had it easy."

And now he is having to walk through a riot when really he feels like a bit of peace and quiet to compose a poem and maybe have a chat with Pearl.

But his optimism immediately reasserts itself. Lux is very, very optimistic. Lux is in fact the most optimistic person that ever lived.

"And love's the burning boy," he mumbles.

3

"LET'S STOP arguing and go to bed," suggests Patrick, and Mike agrees.

"Where is the KY jelly?"

They hunt the flat.

There is no KY jelly to be found.

"That's funny," says Mike, "I bought a giant-size tube just the other day. Where's it gone?"

"Lux!" explodes Patrick. "I saw him with it. He must have been setting his hair with it again!" Sure enough, there in the living room they find the evidence. Lux has squeezed the whole tube of lubricating jelly into a breakfast cereal bowl, mixed in some sugar and gelled his hair with it.

The bowl is stuffed under a chair along with a comb filled with the sticky mixture.

Patrick is livid.

"How could he use the whole tube?" he rages. "Now we can't even fuck because that little monster has set his hair with our jelly. This is your fault. You invited him into the house."

"Calm down," says Mike. "We can use something else." He hunts for some moisturising cream.

When they find out that Lux, always keen to keep his skin looking nice, has used up their new bottle bought only last week from Tesco, Patrick is utterly livid and they lurch back into a dreadful argument, full of personal details and scurrilous suggestions.

Lux, hair set in a spectacular red and yellow forest fire around his head, skin looking very young and smooth, finds that he has reached an impassable roadblock. On his side of the road are masses of rioters. Separated by some burning cars are hordes of police. The rioters throw stones and petrol bombs. The police throw them back and beat on their riot shields with their truncheons, trying to unnerve the rioters prior to making an advance.

Lux looks on, wondering what it is all about.

"What's it all about?" he asks the nearest person. The nearest person looks at him like he is crazy.

Lux tries to peer over the crowd, looking for Pearl. Small, he has difficulty gaining a clear view over all the heads and riot shields. She could be only yards away and he wouldn't see her.

His heart starts to ache.

What I need here is a little help. A group of people he recognises shuffle closer, bricks in hand.

"Help me look for Pearl."

"Drop dead, Lux."

It is a section of the local anarchist collective. They do not like Lux because he laughed so much about them putting up a silly candidate in the last general election. Lux thought he was meant to laugh, he never realised it was serious.

"She might have been kidnapped by police or fascists," he says, trying to interest them. It is useless. They are too busy jostling for position to throw their bricks.

18

"Well I'm glad I never voted for you," shouts Lux at the departing figures. "Don't count on my help in any future struggle."

They don't hear him.

Meeting the anarchists diverts Lux into a slight fantasy.

"What has happened to Pearl Kropotkin?" he mutters. "Kidnapped by secret police and fascists as part of the class struggle? Tortured by spies for information? Only Lux can sort things out . . ."

He goes on hunting.

The smell of smoke is everywhere, slightly troubling Lux, who has an exceptionally acute sense of smell.

"Either he goes or I go," says Patrick, with finality. "He just doesn't fit in with our household."

Mike is glum. He doesn't want to see Lux thrown out onto the street. But as good sex is all that holds him and Patrick together and Lux now seems to be an obstacle in the way of good sex, he is forced to agree.

Kalia is reincarnated in one poor peasant village after another till she starts to feel that she is being persecuted. As far as she understands it these reincarnations should be random and she should at some time be reincarnated as a rich princess or something, enabling her to do a lot of kindness by just giving away money. But no, she is always a peasant. It seems to her that someone in Heaven is trying to make it even more difficult for her and this feeling is magnified when many of her good deeds start to go wrong.

When she piles up firewood outside the home of an elderly priest, the priest trips over it and breaks his neck.

Helping to dig a new well, she turns her back for a moment and a child falls in and drowns. Oh dear, she thinks, fleeing the village pursued by the irate family. Do these still count as acts of kindness? She hopes they do. With another eight hundred thousand still to go she is already fed up with having to act as the country's greatest saint.

But she can't give up. She must get back into Heaven. After living in Heaven, Earth is unbearably tedious. She hates it.

As the police draw near a vicious mêlée breaks out and the sky fills with rocks and stones and flying glass and Lux is wondering which way to go when a half brick hits him behind the ear and he falls down.

The police are dragging away everyone they can lay their hands on so he has to leap to his feet and run despite feeling dizzy and shaken from the blow. Several corners later he has to stop to rest and crouches under a hedge, feeling sick.

AS KALIA'S LIVES wore on she found that she would occasionally meet the same people again, themselves now reincarnated. She used to enjoy these meetings as they gave her some sort of relief from the dreadful loneliness brought about by everyone she knew always dying while she had to go on living, even though none of the souls remembered her in their new reincarnations. Only Kalia is born again and again with memories intact.

She learned how to recognise them by the colour of their aura and the shape of their spirit, things she picked up here and there. One person she met quite a few times, in various incarnations, was Lux, and he was always quite entertaining.

She encountered him in Athens in 420 BC where she was a slave at the theatre and he was always hanging around trying to get sponsors to put on his plays or publish his lyric poems. He never managed it.

"It is a terrible injustice," he complained to her. "The rich patrons are falling over themselves to sponsor Aristophanes and everyone knows I can write Aristophanes under the table any day of the week. Any time I am invited home to discuss business by a rich patron he ends up trying to seduce me on a couch. These people have no morals."

Kalia tries to do him a good turn by bringing him to the attention of her rich master but it turns out badly when Lux is suspected of being a Spartan spy because of his long hair and has to flee quickly, never to be heard of in classical Athens again.

Kalia felt envious of people like Lux who could just have a good time because she never could. Of course she was on her way back to the splendours of Heaven and Lux was doomed to be eternally reincarnated because his spirit would never be in a fit state to be admitted into Heaven, in fact after several of his more degenerate lives he is lucky not to be sent back to Earth as a bug, but as he never knew anything about it this never bothered him. Only Kalia is going through eternity with all her past-life memories intact.

Her loneliness increases. On Earth she comes to hate the people she has to help as they are largely stupid and brutal and any time she meets someone she likes they die after only one short life and then she is lonely again.

To make matters worse, her acts of kindness continue to backfire, as when Lux is denounced as a spy. Someone always seems to be on hand to spoil them. She begins to suspect that her enemies in Heaven have sent down an agent to frustrate her efforts.

A week or so before the riot, Nicky, old friend of Pearl's, turns up at her house looking for sanctuary.

She is so upset that Pearl has difficulty piecing together her story. "I have decided not to let them artificially inseminate me," she says eventually, utterly distressed. "I need a place to hide for a while."

"Who is trying to inseminate you?"

"My employers. Happy Science."

"Are employers allowed to do this sort of thing these days?" asks Pearl, knowing that the government had brought in a lot of new anti-worker legislation.

"I signed a contract with them. I was blackmailed into it by Dr. Carlson."

So Pearl gives Nicky sanctuary although she feels that really she has enough to do already, what with trying to finish her film while desperately warding off Lux, the social security, and the man at the bank who looks after the overdraft she was allowed to build up as a student.

When Lux comes back to his senses after being hit by the brick the riot seems to have raged on to another spot and the street is relatively quiet. There is blood all down his neck and shoulder from the wound on his head and he decides that he had better go home and clean it up before carrying on his search in case an ambulance decides to whip him away for treatment and he ends up confined to a hospital bed.

Possibly Mike and Patrick will come out with him to help him look. He knows that they are a friendly couple. Making his way up Brixton Hill he finds it still relatively trouble free and reaches his temporary home.

When he lets himself in he almost trips over a small bag in the hallway. Why, that is nice of them, thinks Lux. They've tidied up all my stuff into a little bag for me. How thoughtful.

"Hello Patrick. I've just been out in the riot. Pearl's house burned down and I had to rush in and save her, I got hit by the roof falling on me but I managed to save her and I didn't get hurt very much except a girder cut me on the head. Anything interesting happening here?"

"Yes. You're leaving."

"What?"

"You're moving out."

Lux is astonished.

"Why?"

"Because I'm sick of you, you little brat. You use everything in the flat. Since you've been here you've been nothing but a parasite and now you've stolen all our lubricating jelly and moisturising cream."

Lux is upset. He realises, in a flash, that Patrick doesn't like him. This is a shock because he never usually realises that anybody doesn't like him.

23

"I never used the jelly," he lies. "I gave it to some needy child outside to put on his bicycle chain."

"Don't lie, it's all over your hair."

Damn, thinks Lux. Normally a talented liar, the shock of being hit by a brick has made him come out with an unconvincing story.

"I might have used a little bit," he admits. "Would you like me to scrape some off for you?"

"No."

"I'm sure I could manage to give you some back."

"No thank you. I don't intend to fuck through a layer of your hair dye."

"It wouldn't do you any harm. I'll scrape off a clean bit."

It is no use. Patrick, sexually frustrated, is not to be reasoned with. Also Lux's hair, attractive from a distance, is, close up, an incredible mass of various gels and home-made setting agents and Patrick figures it would probably give him a disease that would be impossible to explain at the clinic.

"Get out," he says. "Take your toy robot and Star Wars toothbrush and never come back."

Lux leaves, sadly, clutching the carrier bag. It is at least a well-designed carrier bag in pleasant colours, not like the monstrosities some shops give you. Lux, despite losing his collection, is still a carrier bag fan.

Sebastian Flak is Deputy Chief Accountant at Happy Science PLC and he is not a happy man. He is frustrated because he has not been headhunted by a major American company to be a chief executive somewhere.

Ever since one of his fellow acountants, a man below him in the company hierarchy, was sought out by General Motors to run their European division, Sebastian has been feeling miserable, unappreciated and overlooked.

"Why haven't they headhunted me," he thinks, sadly flicking the pages in his *Soldier of Fortune* mercenary magazine which he has concealed behind a copy of the *Financial Times*. I am a brilliant accountant. Also I am a man of action. Someone must have been spreading bad stories about me.

He has an idea that this someone might be Dr. Carlson, head of the genetic research programme and an important man in the company.

Downstairs Lux knocks on the door of the Jane Austen Mercenaries.

Eugene, the singer, lets him in.

The Jane Austen Mercenaries are friendly to Lux because he has told them, quite untruthfully, that he has started doing gig reviews for a music paper and is just waiting for the right opportunity to write them a good review and make them stars. Lux tells Eugene about saving Pearl from the burning house along with the four children that were trapped on the roof and asks if he can wash the blood off his head and Eugene says yes, but when Lux asks if the singer will come out and help him search for Pearl Eugene says he can't although he is just going down into Brixton for a while to look at the riot. But if Lux will stay a while and look after their guitars he is welcome to wash his wound.

Eugene takes off the comfortable jersey he wears in the house, puts on his leather jacket, and leaves.

Every day Sebastian waits expectantly by the phone, hoping that Ace Headhunters or We Get Your Man Executive Personnel Ltd will phone him up to arrange a secret meeting in a park somewhere where he will be told that General Motors or IBM is after him and how much salary would he like, but so far it hasn't happened, despite Sebastian spreading it around discreetly at business luncheons that he could be tempted away by the right offer.

He has some accounting to do but he is bored with it so he gets back to his mercenary magazine and notes with pleasure that at last there is a really effective portable one-man-operated anti-aircraft missile on the market.

He sees a picture of himself, sent by a major company to sort out a spot of bother with a subsidiary in Central Africa, a sheet of creative accounting notepaper in one hand and a portable missile in the other, bringing down a communist jet fighter whilst simultaneously putting the company back into high profit margins. If that happened then he might get a special profile done on him by *Business Week*. He would like that.

Lux washes off the blood and feels better.

Time to get back out and look for Pearl.

He feels a little fatigued.

What's this bundle of white powder lying on the table?

Tasting it he finds it is cocaine.

Lux figures they will not notice a little bit missing and anyway they owe him a favour as he is going to review them for a music paper and it will give him some energy for searching, so he rolls up a piece of paper and starts to separate a small line with a kitchen knife, but just at that moment there is the sound of a violent struggle and a policeman bursts through the door wrapped in combat with a rioter.

Oh dear, thinks Lux, and starts sniffing frantically, knowing that more policemen will be in hot pursuit. The constable and the civilian crash round in the hall and more heavy footsteps sound outside. Lux snorts away furiously, desperate not to be arrested for cocaine when he has to get out looking for Pearl. When his nose is totally congested he lowers his head to the table and eats what is left, licking his tongue over the mirror till no trace of the drug remains.

"Sorry to disturb you like this," says the policeman, now handcuffing the man as some others appear. "We've chased this coon all the way down the street and I wasn't going to let the bastard go."

"Right," says Lux, eyes starting to glaze.

"Take care of yourself," says the policeman, remembering his Community Training Programme.

Lux, of course, young artist, does not like policemen bursting in being insulting about coons but he is not going to argue with them as he discovered long ago that the best you get for arguing with a policeman is a trip to the police station.

The constables leave. Huge lumps of cocaine start pouring down Lux's nasal passages. A breeze blows in the shattered door. Temporarily forgetting what he is meant to be doing, Lux strums on a guitar, picking out the notes with his perfect nails.

"I wonder if I'll get another house," says Pearl. It took her two years' membership of a housing co-op to get the one that has just been burned down. Nicky makes no reply and Pearl leads her on, one arm round her friend and the other round her bag of salvaged possesions.

Pearl's prize possession, virtually the only thing that she saved, is a roll of film, a film that she has spent almost a year making with some friends from art school.

Making an independent film is almost impossibly difficult. The print in her hand is the only one in existence. Badly harassed and somewhat frightened by the increasing violence around her, Pearl will nonetheless kill anyone who tries to lay their hands on it.

Lux suddenly feels that he is on top of the world. He often feels like this so it does not really strike him that it is the massive dose of cocaine working its way round his body.

At five feet three inches Lux does not have a lot of body for it to work round. He is small everywhere. Although he thinks his legs are perfect like Betty Grable's they are really a little bit thinner. Still, they are good legs. Often he wears short trousers to show them off and then he is whistled at by men on scaffolding and when they realise he is male they shout abuse at him. And, he muses, I am getting pretty good on the guitar. I wonder if I could steal one somewhere.

Being seventeen, hopelessly in love, and maniacally vain, it would be natural if Lux was a terrible poet. But in fact he is quite a good poet which makes it hard for him that no one ever wants to listen to his poems, except occasionally Pearl, who has a kind heart, sometimes.

He makes up strange cut-up verses in his head, shuffling around the lines like beads on an abacus till they fall in place to his satisfaction. Inside Lux's head is a literary computer, unwanted by the rest of the world.

No publication has ever published anything he has sent them, or even talked kindly of it. Nobody has ever really said to him that he has any talent. But Lux is not downhearted by this because he is too optimistic to be downhearted even when the *Times Literary Supplement* went out of their way to send him a special letter saying please don't send us any more poems and *Uptown* tried to pretend to him that they had changed their address.

Lux is at least loved by animals. Dogs and cats follow him around in packs, which he likes. Sometimes he speaks to them. He feels that they appreciate his work.

Hunting round in the flat for a while he finds some make-up and touches up his face, a little pale from loss of blood, thinking that he can't disappoint his public by appearing out on the streets looking bad, also there might be more TV cameras about.

He knows it is only a matter of time until he is a star of some sort and he wouldn't like some cheap tabloid to publish a bad photo of him taken at an unfortunate moment.

Then he comes across the Jane Austen Mercenaries' demo tape, a tape that has caused him some distress due to the band playing it over and over again at massive volume when he is trying to sleep upstairs.

Aha, he thinks.

At work, Nicky never got on very well with anyone else in Happy Science but she made very good friends with her computer.

She doesn't get on very well with anyone because she is the sort of person who just can't see the joke when a strange man in a pub tells her that she has nice tits. So with all the fun-loving young executives and computer operatives in Happy Science happy to say this sort of thing all the time while she is trying to get on with her work she never reacts well and is never really popular.

Still she is very good at her work and Dr. Carlson promotes her in the department and lets her help with the genius project, even proudly showing her the frozen sperm collected from all the nation's geniuses, although Nicky does not manage to sound as enthusiastic about this as he might like. But generally most people leave her alone except for Sebastian Flak, who is particularly keen on her.

She starts to form a deep bond with her computer.

Lux does not like the Jane Austen Mercenaries. He thinks they are crass and unpleasant sounding. Also he thinks they are sexist. Lux's sexual politics are now very good, because if he ever came out with anything bad Pearl would clap him round the head and he learns quickly when he is being clapped round the head.

As well as this they have refused his persistent offers to write lyrics for them.

At the last count fourteen Brixton bands have refused Lux's persistent offers to write lyrics for them.

He puts the demo tape in his carrier bag along with three more copies lying on the floor.

Now so wrecked as to be totally irresponsible he takes a lipstick and writes on the wall:

> *dear jane austen mercenaries, thank you for letting me get*
> *washed in your flat. a policeman broke down the door. do*

not worry about your drugs i managed to finish them all before they were discovered. you can repay me the favour some other time. i am taking your demo tape because it is an insult to the nation's ears. if you would like me to write you some good lyrics, get in touch.

    lux

Making sure that his notebook is handy in case he feels a poem coming on, Lux sets off again, heart starting to ache because Pearl is struggling along somewhere without him.

A WEEK BEFORE the riot Mary Luxembourg the novelist phones up Gerry at his desk at the offices of *Uptown*.

Mary Luxembourg is soaring up the alternative bestseller charts with her first novel, largely due to the wonderful full-page review that Gerry gave her.

Mary Luxembourg is Gerry's hero.

A wonderful feminist classic, he called it, full of startling imagery and memorable characters involved in a long dream of freedom.

The book is now being picked up on by the straight press, whose book editors would not like to be thought of as old fogeys.

"Gerry," says Mary, after Gerry has finally answered the phone, "My publisher is clamouring for the next one. It is all thanks to your review. Next week I am being interviewed by the *Sunday News*."

"The workers are on strike at the *Sunday News*," replies Gerry. "It is being put out by the management and scab labour. Should a left-wing feminist author be talking to them?"

"I need the publicity," says Mary. "And anyway it will spread the message among people who would otherwise not hear it. And also I will put a good word in for you with their book editor so that he will read your novel when it comes out. How is it coming along?"

"Pretty well," replies Gerry, "I have some startling imagery in it. And some notable characters. It is sort of a long dream of freedom."

"Sounds terrific. Incidentally, can I have the manuscript of my new novel back?"

"I haven't finished it yet."

"I need it. I've lost the only other copy. It was stolen out of my Audi."

Gerry's heart sinks. He knows that he has lost the manuscript. He manages to keeps calm.

"I'll drop it right round," he says blithely. "Bye."

Gerry considers the situation. It seems bad. He has lost the only copy of Mary Luxembourg's new novel and this could be a terrible blow to his credibility because he is always going on at his friends about what a wonderful novelist she is and bragging about how friendly they are. What is more, he is utterly depending on a good quote from Mary Luxembourg for the back of his first novel. It will make all the difference to his sales. Since Mary Luxembourg is becoming a big novelist thanks to his reviews, this seems like a convenient arrangement.

He can't quite remember where he lost the manuscript.

Lux is back in the riot. He has no idea why it is going on.

"Why is there a riot going on?" he asks a stranger, an elderly man who is standing beside him watching some people across the street throwing stones.

"We are suffering more than usual," says the man.

"Oh. Who is?"

"Us. Black people. No jobs, no money, policemen stopping the youth in the street all day."

Lux is concerned to hear this.

"Can I do anything to help?" he asks. But the man doesn't think so, and Lux goes on his way.

Lux, not much in touch with the real world, doesn't really know anything about these things, although in this he is not alone, even among the people who live locally. Like many of the whites in Brixton he co-exists with the blacks without actually knowing much about what is going on among them, and if a sixteen-year-old black is stopped and questioned by the police five times in one day, it doesn't make the TV news.

Still, he doesn't quite understand why anyone would riot if they couldn't get a job. Lux would be more inclined to riot if he had to get one. He looks around to ask the man, but he has disappeared.

"Have you seen Pearl?" he asks some more complete strangers, expecting that they will have.

"Pearl who?"

"Just Pearl," says Lux.

"What does she look like?"

"She has finely textured cropped red hair like blood-soaked grass," he tells them, quoting loosely from one of his poems. No one recognises the description.

Unnoticed by Lux the police on the far corner are about to advance. One last fierce shower of missiles and the crowds in the road retreat, carrying him with them, so that he does not catch a glimpse of Pearl, who was only yards away in the crowd but is now carried off in the opposite direction.

Pearl and Nicky are deposited in a doorway where a moment's peace breaks out.

Nicky breaks out as well in one of the frantic bursts of speech which occasionally pierce her psychotic silence.

"The whole place was a nightmare."

"Where?"

"Happy Science. It was full of madmen. I never understood what they were all up to.

"There was an accountant called Sebastian who was going mad

because he was a failure and read mercenary magazines and chatted me up all day long and my head of department was Dr. Carlson who was going mad as well because his serious scientific project had been taken over by someone called Mr. Socrates in the publicity department who wanted to run a beauty contest to attract public sympathy and stop environmental groups going on about them ruining the countryside all the time. It was a nightmare."

Pearl motions Nicky on and they hurry down the street which is for the time being clear of obstruction though littered with minor riot debris and fast-food cartons.

"Perhaps people riot because they're full of fast-food poison," says Pearl, a little sick of tales of Happy Science which she has already heard many times, but Nicky ignores the interruption.

"Mr. Socrates had huge influence in the company because he had the idea of adding fifty per cent water to all their beauty products and then saying on the labels that they were now fifty per cent purer. They thought he was a genius. I would have resigned because they are so stupid but I'm in so much debt I need the money. Where are we going?"

"Somewhere safe."

Kalia's acts of kindness start to go more and more wrong. She can hardly sweep a floor without someone tripping over her and breaking their collarbone. When she saves food to give to holy men it turns out to be rotten and poisons them. For a while there are no healthy priests left in the province.

When she is reincarnated as an Eskimo almost the first thing she does after learning to walk is to sharpen up her father's harpoons but when he comes to use them they have been mysteriously weakened and he is eaten by a walrus.

Someone is definitely dogging her footsteps. Her enemies in Heaven have sent someone down to Earth to make sure she never gets back.

Pearl is slightly lame in one foot. She always wears strong boots. Lux now likes women in boots.

They run into another fierce patch of rioting and Nicky becomes blank again. Struggling through the riot, Pearl's foot hurts, so they take temporary refuge behind a huge crowd of people, onlookers. All round there are people rioting and people onlooking and sometimes the rioters cross over into the other crowd for a rest and sometimes an onlooker gets worked up and joins the rioters and sometimes people are somewhere in between onlooking and rioting, but everywhere the police are forming up into impenetrable phalanxes prior to clearing the streets because by now they are well used to this sort of thing and specially trained to deal with it.

Another camera crew hoves into sight, shrouded in smoke from the burning buildings.

Aha, thinks Lux.

"Hello, I'm Lux, an important local poet. Would you like to hear some of my poems?"

"Get the fuck out of here."

"What way is that to speak? I never heard you tell the prime minister to get the fuck out of here. Do you wanna hear a poem or not?"

"No. We're covering the riot."

"It was one of my poems that started it. Would you like to hear it?"

The cameraman would rather kill Lux than hear his poem. Restraining himself from violence he swings round the camera on his shoulder to film some policemen scattering in the face of a petrol bomb attack. The petrol blazes up out of the shattering milk bottles and lights up the fading day with blue and yellow flames.

"Such yellow sullen smokes make their own element," says Lux, pursuing the camera. "That's Sylvia Plath. Now I'll read you one of mine."

Personal Computer Services exists to make sure that businesses using computers don't get any aggravation from anyone. When they hear about the terrible aggravation that Nicky has caused Happy Science they are immediately hot on the trail, hunting her down with the intention of bringing her to justice and also recovering the vital genetic programme without which the nation will crumble, not having a new generation of geniuses to lead it.

Happy Science has predicted that the nation will be particularly short of geniuses very soon because educational standards are falling all the time and nobody has to sit an Eleven Plus exam any more but spends all their time in primary school playing with sandpits and guinea pigs instead of learning the twelve-times table. The education system is practically in ruins.

No wonder we are falling behind in the export market, they tell government committees. No one knows enough any more to export anything. You don't catch them playing in sandpits in Japanese primary schools. In a Japanese primary school everyone is learning the twelve-times table before they can walk. They never get near a guinea pig. Without our genius project we might as well just throw in the towel.

The government committees give them full support and the project races along, until it is ruined by Nicky.

"I need to rest," says Nicky, somewhere between Brixton and Stockwell.

"Me too. What's in that bag?"

"A genetic programme," says Nicky. "And the manuscript for a new novel."

Oh god, thinks Pearl, she really is cracking up.

Pearl is of course not feeling very good with her house being burned down and all her possessions lost. She is not insured. Her guitar is gone and the tapes of music she was trying to knock into shape to get her band going have gone and so have her paintings.

All her artistic endeavours burned by a stray petrol bomb.

Some ashes float into her short red hair. They stain her face. In front of her there seems to be no way through.

Some rioters speak enthusiastically to them about a big attack they are going to make, but Pearl just wants to get down to Kennington where she knows the riot will probably not reach and her friend will give them shelter for a while.

"How come you never have any good programmes on TV?" demands Lux, working his way in front of the camera. "Why didn't you even reply when I sent you a tape recording of me reading poetry?"

"Get the fuck out of here," bawls the cameraman, manoeuvring desperately into position round Lux as a ferocious battle breaks out only yards away, with ten rioters trying to haul back the furiously kick-ing body of a colleague that the police are dragging away.

"Could I get my own TV programme?" says Lux, hopefully, himself desperately manoeuvring round into the viewfinder.

"Go away," scream the crew. "You're ruining all our pictures."

"What're you filming?" asks Lux, too wrecked by now and too involved in the prospect of his own TV programme to remember much about the outside world.

"Lux!" screams a voice from across the road. "Give us back our demo tape. I'm going to fucking kill you."

"Damn," curses Lux, lurching back to reality. "Interrupted at the vital moment. Another minute and I'd've had my own programme."

He scurries off up the street.

Patrick sees him scurry up the street on television as the camera picks out his distinctive figure, hair flying, long coat flapping.

6

JOHNNY IS leading his squadron of trained operatives from Personal Computer Services into the riot zone. He is a popular leader.

Johnny has tattoos over his shoulders and arms, most of them done while he was in the army. He has thick black hair cut short and a small moustache. He is popular with his friends because he has a fund of good stories and tells them well in the pub. There is the one about wanking in an armoured car in Belfast, the one about going to a disco and picking up a girl in a wheelchair, wheeling her home and taking her off the wheelchair in the park to fuck her, the one about how he ran his car at a nigger in the road and made him fall in a puddle, the one about how when he was a police-cadet he pushed his truncheon up the vagina of a prostitute they had in for questioning.

He is a great storyteller.

Lux, nimble despite his head wound, shins over a wall to escape from Eugene. Along with Eugene is Grub, one of the Jane Austen Mercenaries' four guitarists.

"I'll kill the little bastard," says Grub, flexing his muscles in his filthy leather jacket. "He's took every copy of the demo tape."

They keep searching. Their tape going missing is a disaster. Just that evening they had a phone call from a record company where an executive has been listening to the riot on the radio. The executive knows that Brixton will be big news for a while, and he has a vague memory of receiving some tape from a band in Brixton. Sure enough, when he hunts around in the drawers where he stuffs all the tapes that get sent to him he finds the demo from the Jane Austen Mercenaries.

At least he finds the cover, but when he plays it he finds that he has taped some of his Beatles favourites over it. Never mind, he knows they will have another copy. I must sign them up for a quick single, he thinks. If I get it out immediately it will sell.

Eugene, receiving the call, is ecstatic about this attention from a record company but a little distressed to find that all their tapes have gone, along with their cocaine.

The band set out to look for Lux. When they find him they will recover the tapes and probably give him a good kicking as well, which will not be bad for their image.

Kalia's guess that someone has been commissioned by her enemies in Heaven to frustrate her return is correct. Yasmin, assassin, has been sent to dog her every move with instructions to ruin her efforts, wreck her acts of kindness, make her position so hopeless that she will eventually give up.

He arrives on Earth around 800 B.C. and immediately starts giving her a hard time. The minor prince in the heavenly palace who framed her is frightened that if she returns, now a creditable being who cannot be ignored having performed the million good acts, she may be able to prove that it was him who was the real villain of the heavenly coup.

Seeing Kalia getting on so well with the kindness he sends Yasmin down to stop her. Yasmin, a nasty piece of work who only got into Heaven because the prince forged his Karmic record in return for services rendered, began to plague Kalia's every lifetime. The rate of good deeds completed slumped dramatically and Kalia, seeing endless lifetimes of hopelessness stretching out in front of her, began to feel depressed and defeated.

Now, however, wandering around in the riot doing acts of kindness to everyone who needs one, she is cheered up to see a figure she recognises. It is Lux.

For some days after Mary Luxembourg's call Gerry casts around desperately trying to find what he has done with the manuscript. Finally it strikes him that he left it at the house of a girl called Nicky he was trying to pick up after a Nicaragua benefit gig in Brixton Town Hall. It might be a little embarrassing seeing her again as she threw him out the house, not wanting to fuck him, but at least now he can get it back.

During this time he is in a terrible mood and every review he does is killing. Any film or book unfortunate enough to come under his scrutiny is destroyed outright and everyone else at *Uptown* goes very gently around him because they know that if they rub him up the wrong way then he will denounce them as oppressors and they all hate to be denounced as oppressors, particularly by someone who is such good friends with Mary Luxembourg, the novelist of the moment.

Once denounced as an oppressor by *Uptown* magazine there is no way back. Everyone knows that if they don't like you there must be something pretty badly wrong with you.

"My father hated me," mumbles Nicky, sheltering with Pearl behind a wall.

"Right," says Pearl. "We should be able to work our way through if we head on towards Stockwell."

"Everybody made fun of me at university."

"Right."

"You're not listening."

"I'm trying to get us to somewhere safe."

"I don't care if we're safe. I'd as soon be dead. I might kill myself anyway. I killed my computer. My only friend."

"Oh thanks," says Pearl.

"My only friend apart from you. Everyone else hates me."

"No they don't."

"Yes they do. Lux wrote a terrible poem about me on the wall."

"That wasn't Lux. He isn't vindictive. Anyway, I'd recognise his handwriting."

"He still hates me. He's jealous of us. Personal Computer Services are coming to get me."

"There is no such thing as Personal Computer Services."

"Even you don't believe me," says Nicky, wide-eyed. "They do exist, they're evil. It was them that assassinated the man who broke into the Queen's bank account. Now they're after me and they're after you as well, because of the film."

"What?"

Nicky falls silent and won't speak any more.

Wonderful, thinks Pearl, and pokes her head out to see if the coast is clear.

A phalanx of policemen is marching up the road. They take cover again.

Pearl has been going to self-assertiveness classes where they have taught her how to shove her way through aggressive strangers and frighten them off by using her voice powerfully. As far as she can remember there was no class telling you how to deal with forty aggressive policemen. Possibly that was next term.

"What's that smell?" says Nicky.

"My organic moisturising cream," replies Pearl.

"I recognise that smell," thinks Lux, who has a very acute sense of smell. It is Pearl's natural organic moisturising cream. She must be somewhere close.

I recognise that aura, muses Kalia.

"Hello Lux."

"Hello."

"Nice to meet you again."

"Right," says Lux, not having any idea who Kalia is but never willingly impolite.

"I haven't seen you for a few hundred years. Not since the Spanish Inquisition, if I remember correctly. What are you doing?"

"Hunting for Pearl. Do you want to help?"

"Certainly," says Kalia, and joins in the search.

Johnny, now in hot pursuit of Nicky and Pearl, joined the police after leaving the army. He loved it at the police college, where they taught him how to work his police radio and how to drive a car fast with the siren going neeneneene and how to deal with coons without starting riots all the time.

But due to a terrible injustice he was thrown out of the force almost as soon as he settled in when he had the dreadful misfortune to beat up a black student who was staying in the country with a family of rich whites. The rich whites made a terrible fuss and Johnny was expelled.

Since then his life has been hard. He no longer has big wages and has had to sell his car, which caused him great distress because he firmly believed that a big car was very good for impressing women, in fact he thinks that his recent lack of success with women may be due to his not having such a big car any more.

But now, re-employed by Personal Computer Services because of all his valuable experience, he has a chance to start all over again. He is determined not to foul it up. He will bring back the genetic programme if he has to kill Nicky to get it.

"Well," says Mark, "if we're going to Brixton we might as well leave."

"I should finish these book reviews first," says Gerry. "I have a volume here that has been cited all over as the major novel of the decade."

"It's getting late."

"Is it? Oh fuck it then." He sweeps the novel of the decade into the bin. "It is probably trash anyway. Let's go."

When Pearl crouches down she puts her hand out to lean on and makes contact with a still dribbling condom.

Terrific, she thinks, shaking her hand.

One time she went to a party and some students played a game of putting condoms over their heads and blowing them up. The game was called Horses. To Pearl it didn't seem like a lot of fun but it gave the students hours of enjoyment.

Thinking of the party makes her think of Lux because he was there, trying to write a poem on the kitchen wall with a red crayon until the person who lived there found out and threatened to throw him out of the window.

"What d'you mean throw me out the window," protested Lux. "I'm doing you a favour. When I'm world champion poet this kitchen wall will be worth a lot of money. People will come from miles to see it. Probably TV crews will come to make programmes about it."

Lux has some vague and confused notion about being world champion poet, picked up during some drunken reading of a newspaper report about some obscure poetry contest.

"I know plenty of poetry," he told Pearl. "As well as writing my own I know bits from Homer and Sappho down to ee cummings and Stevie Smith. I could quote you the whole of Milton's *Paradise Lost*."

"Go on then," said Pearl.

"It's slipped my memory. Still, I am a prime candidate for world champion poet. You'll be sorry you wouldn't sleep with me when I'm being interviewed on breakfast television and photographed for the *Reader's Digest*."

44

"I did sleep with you."

"Only partially," replied Lux, dragging up an old argument. "Your heart wasn't in it. I don't reckon it counted."

The only time that, to Kalia's knowledge, Lux ever had any success in life is when in twelfth-century Japan he turned out to be a spectacular success at the perfume guessing game.

With no warfare going on, the Japanese aristocracy sit around all day being civilised and playing games and one of their favourites is perfume guessing, in which various aromas are offered round blind and they have to guess what they are.

Lux, turning up as usual in a kimono that has seen better days and a hairstyle that would probably get him beheaded by a samurai were it not for him being an artist and therefore allowed some degree of liberty, begs some food from the rich household in return for his poems. Possibly because he is more than usually hungry he does not declaim any of his own works and sticks to the classics, so he is quite well received and, full up with rice and fish, is invited to play the game.

He amazes everyone with his skill. He is sensational at guessing perfumes.

The household invite him to stay a while as they have an important perfume-guessing contest coming up soon with some rivals from the next hamlet.

Gerry and Mark make it to Brixton later in the evening, having had to get off the tube several stations early and walk the rest of the way.

Outside the riot they are stopped by the police but when they say they live in the area and have to get home they are let through.

Brixton Road is now fairly clear and the riot, though still growing in intensity, has moved sideways into the streets and estates. A police helicopter flies deafeningly overhead and more and more buses of police crawl into the area, green single-deck buses full of officers from other areas.

Almost immediately they meet Lux, who is standing adjusting his hair in front of the remains of a shop window while Kalia stands around watching.

The window belongs to a butcher's shop. As a vegetarian he is not sorry to see it wrecked. Eating animals makes him feel upset.

"Hello," says Gerry. They know each other through having met at Pearl's when Gerry was visiting Nicky.

"Hello," says Lux, without enthusiasm. He does not like Gerry because *Uptown* refused to publish any of his poems. Although Gerry didn't have anything to do with the decision Lux regards him as working for the enemy.

"We're going round to Pearl and Nicky's."

"No use," says Lux, and tells them that the house is burned down and he is just now searching for them.

"Damn. The house burned down. Did they save the manuscript?"

"No," replies Lux, despite not having any idea what manuscript Gerry is talking about. "All they had left when I handed them out through the window to the firemen was the clothes they were wearing and a book of my poems. There wasn't time to save anything else."

"Where are they now?"

"I don't know. They drove off in the fire engine."

"Did you see the riot start?" asks Gerry.

"No." Lux shakes his head, fairly violently, body tingling with the cocaine. "I just walked out of the house and it was going on. I don't even know what it is about."

Gerry gives him a look of contempt.

"It's anti-police oppression and racism and the repressive state of the nation," he tells him.

"Right," agrees Lux. "I am pleased to know. I got hit by a brick. I wasn't doing any oppressing at the time."

"Well you should have got out of the way," says Gerry. "Anyway, there will be innocent casualties. Although you are probably not that innocent."

Lux thinks of Pearl being an innocent casualty and becomes frantic again.

7

THRASH METAL guitarist Grub, man of action, chases round after Lux with Eugene. Grub has a degree in astro-physics from Cambridge University but, unlike his guitar, keeps it quiet.

The other three members of the band are back at the flat, guarding the instruments from the riot in case anyone decides to riot through their shattered door.

Lux is nowhere to be found but the two hunt with the sheer determination of any struggling musicians who see the prospect of imminent success. Nothing is going to stop them from getting their demo tape to the record company and putting out a record. They would commit murder to put a record out.

As far as Sebastian could see he was at a dead end in Happy Science. Although an important company it was not the sort of business that rates deputy accountants very highly and he realised that without some high profile exposure he was never going to come to the attention of IBM or Coca Cola and they would never send a headhunting company after him with a big offer.

The only good thing in his life is Maybeline, brought over from the

USA to be chief computer programmer. Sebastian has been talking to her and she seems to like him.

Sebastian might like Happy Science better if he was party to the secret plan being formulated to genetically code everyone in the country and make sure that only nice people have babies, or the illegal Happy Science genetic experiments which are going to make them the company of the future, but these plans are being kept quiet in case rival companies steal them. So it seems to Sebastian that Happy Science is a dead end.

Lux talks to Gerry for a time while Kalia hunts in her pockets for ten pence for a passing tramp who is struggling along in urine-drenched confusion but is trying not to let the riot affect his income.

Eugene and Grub appear round the corner.

"Bye," says Lux, nipping through a garden and over another wall, band in pursuit.

"What do you think that was about?"

Gerry shrugs. "No doubt he's stolen something off them. I've heard he is light-fingered."

Kalia finds ten pence for the tramp and leaves.

Gerry wonders what to do about the lost manuscript. It is a disaster any way you look at it. Mary Luxembourg's copy has been stolen and his copy has been burned in a fire. He will never be able to hold his head up at *Uptown* again after Mary Luxembourg denounces him. Unless of course no one particularly cares about her any more.

"Quick. We have to find a phone."

"We'll never get through this way," says Pearl, exasperated. "I wish these people would all fuck off and let me get out of here. Come on, let's try this way."

"He used to try and make other companies employ him," mumbles Nicky. "It was pathetic."

"What?"

"A close escape," mutters Lux, having evaded the Jane Austen Mercenaries. "Closer than the time Patrick demanded I went shopping with him and helped cook a meal."

"Well, well, look what the cat dragged in," says a voice full of husky sensuality.

"Hello John," says Lux. "Nice dress. Have you seen Pearl?"

John yawns, deliberately.

"Stop pursuing that female, Lux. You're wasting your time."

They look at each other. John, in his dress and high heels, has known Lux for a while but their friendship has never really got much beyond swapping tips about make-up because John is one hundred percent concerned with being gay and in some way regards Lux as a traitor, because Lux is so attractive, wears such nice make-up, but isn't homosexual, or not very.

They are standing outside the terrace where John lives, flanked on either side by more people who form a small gay community.

"Hello," screams Tim, John's lover, and grabs Lux up to kiss him in greeting. Lux kisses him back and the process takes quite a long time.

"We're having a riot party. I've just been collecting the Judy Garland records. Will you stay?"

"I have to look for Pearl."

John and Tim both yawn, dramatically.

They are very camp, unlike Mike and Patrick. Lux is not keen on campness and thinks he should be on his way.

"Some people were asking after you. Some musicians."

"Wanting me to write them a new song again?" suggests Lux brightly.

"I don't think so. Sure you won't stay for the party?"

"I've got to find Pearl. She is alone in the riot."

"I knew there would be a riot," says John, adjusting his hemline. "The socio-economic factors were exactly right for—' He stops as Tim digs him in the ribs. "Sure you wouldn't like to hear some Judy Garland?" he finishes.

"No thank you," says Lux, and walks on.

He likes Judy Garland but right now he is a man with a mission.

It was a moment of maniacal genius when Sebastian struck upon the idea of creating some market interest in himself.

"Hello. Is that Ace Headhunters? I am speaking on behalf of Coca Cola." He puts on an American accent. "We're looking for a new man to run our South American operation. He has got to be someone exceptional, capable of clearing rainforests in Brazil and building sales figures in Chile. Is there anyone suitable you could get for us. Who's that? Never heard of him."

Sebastian dismisses all the proffered suggestions.

"These are all third-raters. What we need is something special. The Chilean army is a huge Coca Cola market. How about this man Sebastian Flak? We've been hearing a lot about him over here in the States." Sebastian makes a little clicking noise to make it sound like it is a trans-Atlantic telephone call.

The Ace Headhunters agent confesses to never having heard of Sebastian Flak.

"Well in that case we had better try another headhunting company. You are obviously not on the ball."

With that he rings off, satisfied that it is a good start, and takes a turn round the building to see if there are any secretaries or research assistants he can sexually harass for a while as Maybeline is away on a course for the week, learning some advanced management techniques and probably having a good time.

Lux is well treated in the Japanese household. Every day they feed him rice and fish and give him a new kimono and the family lets him read out his own poems which they pretend to like because he is their secret weapon in the perfume guessing game.

They have never beaten the neighbouring hamlet. This counts as a disgrace to their village, but the neighbouring hamlet has a man who is reputed to have a god-given nose and never makes a mistake. In all the time they have been playing the game they have never come across anyone to rival him, except perhaps Lux.

He is put in strict training and spends hours every day sniffing perfumes in unmarked containers while the family coach marks down the results.

"Excellent, excellent," exclaims the coach. "You have a superb nose."

Lux is pleased at the compliment and pleased at the unusual hospitality.

Kalia meanwhile does her duties in the household. The youngest daughter, she is not very important in the family, but after scores of unimportant lives she is used to this and carries on cooking and clean-ing with her usual forced enthusiasm, wondering how many hundreds of thousands of kind acts she has left to complete.

Lying with a Friend under a Burnt-out Truck

Under the burnt-out truck Lux continues to ramble.

"Tonight has been a waste of time. I could've been writing poetry instead of running around in a riot. But people do a lot of things that are a waste of time. Mike and Patrick go surfing. Do you know what surfing is? I saw it on television. You go out to sea on a plank of wood and then you float back to the shore. Then you do it again. Imagine. It is almost as pointless as jumping out of a plane on a parachute.

"Once I knew a girl who worked in a hamburger restaurant. I was horrified. Imagine working in a hamburger restaurant. Do you think they get deliveries of whole cows at the back door and then make them into hamburgers? People do terrible things to cows. It shouldn't be allowed.

"The social security wanted me to get a job. They tried to force me to work in a hamburger restaurant and cut up cows instead of writing poetry. They seemed to think it was more worthwhile. If my signing-on clerk hadn't been crazy about my good looks I'd be up to my elbows in blood at this very moment."

He pauses.

"I keep getting this funny feeling I'm heading naked into battle."

His brilliant red and yellow hair splays all over the tarmac, but under the truck they are hidden from the outside world.

A FEW ACCOUNTANTS come in for a meeting with Sebastian, which frustrates him a little as he is impatient to get on with whipping up interest in himself. Also, he has a new issue of *Soldier of Fortune* to read.

The mercenary magazines have given Sebastian some confusing images when he masturbates. One involves marching into some village in Africa and raping all the women at gunpoint. Another has him making love to some woman who is carrying a Kalashnikov and wearing an army uniform such as he has seen in pictures of the Nicaraguan army.

Sebastian is confused about his sexuality and this surfaces occasionally.

The first time he meets Lux is when the young poet arrives at the door of Happy Science just as the accountant is leaving and demands to be allowed to add his sperm to the genius collection.

"Why?"

"Because I am a genius of course. Also, I came out of a test tube and have experience of this sort of thing. Would you like to hear a poem?"

"No."

"Well is there a genius selection committee? I could read them some of my work. They'd let me in, no bother. How exactly do you collect the sperm? Do you suck it out with a big machine or do you have to have an operation or does everybody just masturbate into a test tube? If so could I bring along a friend to help?"

Sebastian starts to feel a little uneasy. Lux, hair resplendent, trousers ripped to show off his legs, sticks out in the business section of the city like a kind heart at a management meeting. People walking past in their suits are starting to stare and Sebastian is embarrassed.

Worse, he is slightly attracted. "I'm sorry, I can't help you," he says, and walks off briskly, scared that Maybeline might appear and somehow guess that he is not unattracted by Lux.

"I am the first test tube baby to be a nationally recognised poet," calls Lux after the accountant, a little forlornly, but it has no effect. Disappointed, Lux hunts for someone else to volunteer his services to. Ever since Nicky told him about the project he has been keen to do his bit for the next generation.

He thought they would be pleased to have him.

Gerry finds a phone and phones *Uptown*.

"Are you reporting on the riot?" they ask.

"No," he says. "I want to dictate a retrospective re-appraisal of the works of Mary Luxembourg. Are you ready? Right. Mary Luxembourg has been much over-rated in the past by critics unable to see the ultimate unworthiness of her work . . ."

Mike argues and argues with Patrick until he is forced to storm out of the house saying that he is never coming back because he is not willing to share a house with anyone uncharitable enough to turn Lux out into the street in the middle of a riot.

Patrick wishes he had never set eyes on Lux and sits angrily in front of the television, watching game shows interspersed with up-to-the-minute riot reports.

Mike makes his way through the seething streets which is easy in some places, difficult in others. Some side roads are blocked by police, others aren't. Some are pouring with missiles, some aren't. There are not enough rioters or police to entirely fill all of the streets.

He meets a friend who is carrying a leather coat and a pair of jeans liberated from a shop and the friend is very pleased about this because he has not had a new coat for three years. He tells Mike that the main road is presently impassable but if he makes his way along Acre Lane and through the back streets from there he should be able to reach the office of Liberation Computers, his destination.

Well, thinks Gerry, ending his phone call with some satisfaction. That's fixed that. When people read that retrospective on Mary Luxembourg no one will care if she never publishes another novel again.

Of course now he won't be able to get a quote from her for the back cover of his soon-to-be-completed first novel and this is bad, but not so bad as being a pariah among his peers.

They walk into the centre of the riot, turn a corner and come across a group of five young blacks, one of them bleeding from a wound in his head.

"Tell me what's happening," says Gerry, excited.

"Are you serious?" they say, presuming he is some sort of police spy.

"No," he chuckles. "You don't understand. I'm a journalist."

"A white journalist," says one of them, wryly. "Fuck off, white journalist."

"You don't understand. I work for a left-wing magazine . . ."

"Fuck off, white journalist, before we cut your throat."

They leave.

"In any revolutionary movement there will always be reactionary elements," he explains to Mark, who admires him for his knowledge of this sort of thing.

The five youths hide behind a wall. They have just been chased by some policemen and are planning to get their own back. Two policemen are walking towards them. They go tense in readiness, weapons to hand, ready to pounce.

"Hi everyone," says Lux cheerfully, appearing over the wall. "Anyone seen Pearl? She's sort of this height with short red hair and probably carrying a friend."

"What is this?" they demand, staring at Lux, who is looking more than usually strange with blood still seeping out of his wound and KY jelly starting to run over his face, melted from the heat of the burning butcher's shop.

"No one seen her? Oh well. Fancy hearing a poem?"

"Will you get the fuck out of here, you white bumbawally," hisses one of the youths, seeing that Lux is going to ruin the ambush.

Lux becomes indignant. This continual unthinking rejection of his poetry is a little hard to take, particularly when only he stands between the nation and complete barbarism.

"What do you mean get the fuck out of here?" he says, raising his voice. "Let me tell you the poem I was going to read you was pretty fucking good. Now I might not bother."

"Kill him!" screams the leader, totally frustrated at Lux being so stupid. And they might well have done it had not the two pursuing members of the Jane Austen Mercenaries appeared on the scene at that moment, clambering over the wall a lot less nimbly than Lux.

"Where's the tape?" they scream. The police, hearing all the noise, call for help and rush to the scene. Everyone flees.

"You'll all appreciate me one day," shouts Lux over his shoulder, and disappears.

Dr. Carlson and Sebastian Flak do not get on very well.

This is mainly because Sebastian is always telling him to spend less time and money doing research and start making some more profitable products like stay-fresh hamburgers and medically-recommended toothpaste.

"Where is the new toothpaste?" he demands. "We have a team of dentists all ready to make tests showing it leads to fifty per cent less fillings. The report is already written. Mr. Socrates has the TV commercial well in hand. So where's the toothpaste?"

"The new toothpaste can wait. I am carrying out a serious scientific project."

This goes on all the time. Another reason for bad feeling however is that Sebastian is always trying to pick up the doctor's research assistants in the canteen, particularly Nicky. Sometimes he even comes down to the laboratories brandishing free tickets for the Hippodrome.

Finally the doctor confronts him with this and tells Sebastian that if he bothers any more of his assistants then he will complain to the Managing Director and after this they are deadly enemies so that when Sebastian finds that he is not getting on too well in the company he naturally assumes that it is because Dr. Carlson has been spreading stories about him to the directors.

Sebastian, already bitter about his lack of career progress, becomes more frustrated and blames the directors for believing the stories and completely loses the company loyalty they taught him in business school.

He stops accounting altogether and spends all his time reading magazines and dialling up Maybeline's extension.

"I'm just not getting on in the company," he confesses to her.

He finds her soft American accent soothing and easy to confess to. Maybeline, a little bored after her course on management techniques, asks him to join her for lunch.

Meanwhile Dr. Carlson composes a biting memo to the Chairman complaining about Sebastian always hanging around his laboratories troubling the assistants and trying to get them to come out for drinks.

Lux, in flight, is grabbed by a hand and hauled behind a wall.

"I have a good explanation for everything," he begins.

"Don't bother," says Kalia. "You don't need to explain to me. I already know you are a born thief as well as being hopelessly vain."

"How do you know I am a born thief as well as being hopelessly vain?"

"I've met you before in other lifetimes."

"Oh."

They are in a garden that fronts one of the many large houses in the side streets of Brixton.

Only yards away some people are struggling home with some booty looted from the high street, but Lux is not very aware of his surroundings.

"What is your name?"

"Kalia. I expect you want some explanation about me saying I've met you in former lives?"

Lux's mind is too full up with cocaine and Pearl for him to really understand what Kalia is saying. "Not right now. I am too worried about Pearl. I don't seem to be any nearer finding her. I can't find anyone who's seen her. I can't get anyone to listen to a poem."

He becomes slightly maudlin.

"I don't have anywhere to live. I'm being chased by a bunch of dumb thrash metal merchants. Pearl refuses to fall in love with me. Perhaps it was a bad idea to fall in love with her. Plenty of other women like me. Just the other day someone wanted to take me away to a life of luxury but I didn't go because of Pearl. It is hard being in love."

"Maybe you should have taken the life of luxury."

Lux shrugs.

"I didn't really like the person that much. I only went home with her because she said she wanted to hear some of my poems. When I got there she tried to grapple me into bed. This happens to me a lot. People seem to get the wrong impression when I offer to come home with them and read them some poems."

"Yes," says Kalia. "It is hard being an object."

"It would definitely have been more convenient to fall in love with someone who wants to fall in love with me. Much less trouble. Well, I'd better get looking.

'Then on to the Pnyx
With urgent tread
A fearful threat
Hangs over our head,'" he mutters. "Now, who wrote that?"

"Aristophanes."

Lux frowns. "I'm not sure why, but I never liked Aristophanes. Is my hair looking all right?"

"Perfect."

"Good."

Pearl's film is about some women with magic powers who live in an old block of flats.

They kidnap the hero, played by Pearl, and put her through a painful cathartic process which will be liberating in the end but causes her a lot of hardship at the time.

Also, it is about witches being burnt in the seventeenth century. It has been a long process making it without any money.

Lux, however, has been very supportive with help and ideas, and when Pearl needed someone to play the part of a demon scarecrow Lux was a natural choice. Everyone agrees he is a sensational scarecrow although Pearl never lets him read any of the scarecrow poems he writes specially for the part.

"Wasn't I good in your film," says Lux continually.

"Yes," says Pearl. "Shame you couldn't have helped with some money."

Lux has never had any money.

"I heard it rumoured that some headhunting companies were after me with some substantial offers from large American corporations," Sebastian tells Maybeline over lunch, slightly altering the truth. "But it hasn't come to anything."

This last part is true. Despite his best efforts, Sebastian has failed in his bid to generate interest in himself.

"I envy you," he continues. "You have just been promoted. You are obviously heading for success. Everything you do goes well."

"It's all due to chanting," she tells him.

"Chanting?"

"Yes. Every day I chant Nyam Myoho Rengi Kyo for fifteen minutes. It has brought me success. Before I started I was merely a computer programmer and now I am managing the whole department."

Sebastian is interested, if dubious. He can't see himself chanting.

"How does it work?"

Maybeline shrugs. "No one knows. It is a Buddhist technique but you don't have to be a Buddhist to use it. I learned it from my brother back in Dallas. He used to be a down-and-out street artist and now he paints murals for oil companies.

"But chanting? It seems like such a strange thing to do."

"But it brings sucess."

9

KALIA SPENDS several lifetimes without pushing up the balance of kindness at all. Inside she rages against Heaven for making things so unfair for her. Powerless against the evil Yasmin, she has seen her hopes fade. The last person she tried to help, a starving beggar she gave some food to in the central Russian steppes, was torn to death by Mongols after Yasmin led them to believe the food was stolen.

This incident makes her despair. Here she is trying to be kind and what happens? The recipient of her kindness is ripped into four small pieces by wild horses.

Yasmin, helped by his heavenly supporters, always seems to turn up in a more powerful position than her. She is always a peasant or a slave or something, and though her lifetimes of accumulated wisdom sometimes make things easier it is never any help against some brute of a warlord, and there seem to be a lot of brutish warlords about.

Next lifetime, however, she receives an unlooked-for stroke of luck when she is born into a family of wise women in the Hopi Red Indian tribe.

Lux admires some rioters with scarfs tied round their faces but decides against copying it as his face is too nice to tie a scarf round. Every few moments he stops someone to ask them if they have seen Pearl while Kalia waits patiently for him to catch up.

"Someone must have seen her."

"Don't worry," says Kalia. "We'll find her."

"I hope so. I'm aching inside."

"Did you argue with her?"

"Certainly not," says Lux, working his way round a group of people giving away some sort of news-sheet. "We never argued. Even when Pearl was being horrible I was pleasant and cheerful."

This is a lie. They did in fact have an argument, brought on by Lux being insensitive when Pearl was suffering a depression about the film not going well.

"The cameraman does not take me seriously," she complained. "Basically he can't work with women. Woman have always had a hard time in the arts."

Lux nods sympathetically.

"We've no sooner stopped getting burned as witches than cameramen start fouling up our films," she continues. "I'm fed up with being disregarded. No one knows any women filmmakers, philosophers, poets ..."

"I don't know about that," interrupts Lux. "There's Sylvia Plath, my favourite. Then there's Maxine Kumin and Rosemary Dobson and Stevie Smith and Fleur Adcock and Ellen Bryant Voigt—"

"Lux"

"—and Elaine Feinstein and Margaret Atwood and Selima Hill and—

"Lux"

"—and Marianne Moore and Charlotte Mew and Ruth Pitter and—owww!"

Lux is brought to a halt by Pearl yanking his hair. Afterwards she won't speak to him because she thinks he is trying to make fun of her, but really it isn't Lux's fault that he happens to know all the world's poets.

"It isn't my fault if I happen to know all the world's poets," he says. "No reason to get upset."

"Pardon?" says Kalia. "Excuse me, I'm just going to help that young man to his feet."

In a comprehensive and efficient act of kindness she picks up a fallen victim, wipes his face, helps him adjust his dreadlocks back into his big hat, and gathers up a few coins that have rolled out of his pocket before sending him on his way. Unfortunately a watching policeman decides that probably anyone lying on the ground with dreadlocks must have been doing something worth arresting him for, and arrests him.

"Are you in love with anyone?" asks Lux.

Kalia shakes her head. "I got bored with it a thousand years ago."

At the offices of Happy Science Dr. Carlson is arguing bitterly with Mr. Socrates from the publicity department about the perfect-mother contest.

"You don't seem to understand," he explains, patience running out, "that what we have here is a serious scientific study involving years of research, not to mention the purchase of the most obscure pornographic magazines in order to collect the sperm from the nation's geniuses. Some of them were very old. We can't just stuff it into any woman who happens to look nice. We need someone who is genetically correct and also intelligent.

Socrates waves away the objections. He has already explained to the Doctor that they can only continue with the project if they generate public interest in it. No high-profile interest for the company and they are liable to cancel the whole thing. It has already cost a phenomenal amount of money and were it not for the fact that the prime minister has personally spoken out in favour of it it would have been cancelled long ago.

"Furthermore, where is the new toothpaste you were meant to be developing?"

Nicky appears, holding a clipboard, preventing the Doctor from coming out with a cutting reply.

"I've got your results," she says, and hands him the clipboard.

"Don't ogle my staff!" says Dr. Carlson to Mr. Socrates as he stares after her departing figure.

During all this time Nicky is having a progressive mental breakdown because she can't relate to the world at all, but no one is very bothered about this because she is never really very friendly to anyone and if you are never all that friendly then who is going to worry about you having a mental breakdown?

She sits at her computer terminal and talks to it.

Good morning, did you sleep well? That sort of thing.

She does not see her friend Pearl very much because Pearl is putting all her time and energy into making her film, and Nicky resents this a little.

Sebastian, still dubious, but impressed both by Maybeline's success and her confident personality, starts his chanting. He does it in secret, slightly worried that people might think he has got religion, or maybe just lost his senses.

For fifteen minutes each day he chants the mantra, without really believing anything will happen.

Of course he has zero interest in Buddhism, but a lot of interest in success in the material world, and Maybeline said it would work.

Lux and Kalia walk on until they are halted by a policeman who tells them to wait while he searches their pockets for anything they may have looted.

"Don't worry," he says in a strangely friendly tone, "we aren't bothering about dope tonight, just stolen goods."

Not finding any stolen goods on either Lux or Kalia, he lets them pass.

"Though why should I whine," says Lux, "Whine that the crime was other than mine?"

"Very nice," says Kalia. "Yours?"

"No, Gwendolyn Brooks."

They walk on, surrounded by a shallow stream of people, all searched and found to be without stolen goods.

"So," says Kalia, picking her way over the broken glass of a shattered shop window and raising her voice slightly as a siren starts up somewhere close, "you don't remember me at all? Well, never mind, I wouldn't expect you to. But I knew you immediately. The aura around your body never changes. Still going around falling in love with unsuitable women and trying to get people to listen to your poetry?"

"Now you mention it, yes."

Lux's brain clears slightly.

"Who exactly are you?"

"I am Kalia. I have been exiled from Heaven for three thousand years. I am engaged in a quest to regain my rightful place in Paradise. Also, I have an idea that some descendant of Heaven is in danger tonight and I am going to try and help them."

"That's a relief," replies Lux. "For a while I thought you might be connected with the Jane Austen Mercenaries. I heard they were looking for a new drummer."

"Have you seen anyone who might be a descendant of Heaven?"

"Do they have any distinguishing marks? A halo or anything?"

"No. But they might have an aura of magic around them."

"Maybe it's Pearl. She would fit the bill. Unless it's me."

"No, it's not you, although you are fairly magical. I always liked the cheerful way you failed at everything."

"Have we met?"

"Often. But you wouldn't remember."

"No, I have a terrible memory. My mind is all full up with cocaine and poetry. And Pearl."

"Why don't you leave her alone?" says a voice from behind.

"What?" says Lux incredulously, turning round to see what maniac is telling him to leave Pearl alone. He finds a young woman giving him some very unfriendly looks.

"Oh, hello Pat," says Lux, still polite but edging slightly behind Kalia. "How is the woman's refuge doing? You haven't seen Pearl anywhere, have you?"

"No, and I wouldn't tell you if I had," declares Pat. "Everyone's sick of you running round after her. What's the idea of bothering a lesbian? You ought to leave her alone and maybe if you don't we'll throw you in the Thames. And don't send any more of your dumb poems to the refuge. We're not going to put them up on the noticeboard."

She leaves.

Kalia looks at Lux. "Well?"

Lux sighs. "Pearl has already lectured me about it. I still have some bruises. But we did sleep together. Anyway," he brightens up, "I figure this sort of thing doesn't apply to young poets in love. Young poets in love are allowed to do anything. Everyone knows that."

Kalia doesn't agree but she doesn't reply. After her thousands of years of tedium on Earth she rarely argues about anything.

"How do you regain your place in Heaven?" asks Lux.

"I have to do a million acts of kindness?"

"Maybe I could help you with one or two," says Lux, "I'm well known for my acts of kindness."

Pearl has fought off the social security people trying to make her get a job in order to keep on with the film and she is not going to let a riot spoil it all.

She would have been safely through to Kennington and her friend's house by now were it not for the fact that she is having to chaperone Nicky and Nicky is finding it difficult to walk because she feels so guilty about destroying her computer and this brings back more bad memories about Happy Science. When they come across a destroyed electrical goods shop and Nicky finds the remains of a small computer lying mangled and unwanted on the pavement she is reduced to tears.

"Come on," says Pearl.

"Maybe I could fix it."

"It's ruined. Put it down."

The sad occurrence starts Nicky off on more bad memories.

"I hated it at work because every time I wore anything different all the men had to make some comment about it." She mimics their voices: "You're looking nice today. Another funny outfit? That's a bit normal by your standards, isn't it? Smartening up are we?"

Pearl, of course, as Nicky's part-time lover, is normally sympathetic to this sort of thing, but now she is too busy concentrating on avoiding the missiles that are flying fiercely.

Down by Stockwell there is a thick mass of people, young blacks from the council estates and young whites from the local squats, all throwing stones and bottles and petrol bombs and sometimes whole ignited garbage cans at a force of policemen who are retreating, outnumbered.

A girl beside Pearl throws a petrol bomb and it spills over the top of a policeman's riot shield to burn round his helmet and some other policemen beat out the flames and this creates a gap in the ranks and more and more stones and bricks start pounding down onto them.

"Sugar and washing up liquid," says the girl to Pearl. "It's no good just putting petrol in, you have to make it flare up and stick to the skin."

"You know," says Lux. "Tonight I have met two TV crews and neither of them wanted to hear any of my poetry. I can't understand it."

Kalia is temporarily busy, helping a man to his feet and setting him on his way.

"Well Lux, they won't take much notice of you because you are not very important."

"But I am a great poet."

"That isn't very important. Not to them anyway."

Lux finds this depressing. He kicks a stone in his path and it sails down an alleyway.

"Good shot," says Kalia.

"Yep," says Lux, pleased. "I was always a good footballer. I could have played for my school."

"Why didn't you?"

"All the other boys refused to go into the changing rooms with me."

"Why?"

Lux shrugs. "I'm not sure. I think they were jealous of my skill. Look, there's another television crew."

He strides up to them.

"Hello," he says, politely. "I am Lux, head of the local council. Would you like to hear some of my poems?"

"You're not head of the local council. I've just been interviewing him up the road."

Damn, thinks Lux. What a stroke of misfortune.

"Well, the head of the local council is a terrible poet," he says, trying to work the situation to his advantage, "whereas I am a genius. Also, I saved some people from a burning building and then I helped the Jane Austen Mercenaries get a recording contract by writing them some good reviews and now I'm on my way to hospital to give blood as I have a unique blood group and am always on call for saving a few lives when neccessary, so how about letting your listeners hear a decent poem?"

"No."

"Why not?"

"I'm here to report on the riot."

"Who cares about a riot?"

"The whole country."

"Well I don't. I think it's a bore. Have you seen Pearl anywhere? She has a small thin body like an F1-11 jet fighter."

"Please go away."

Lux shuffles away, disappointed, with Kalia, who sympathises.

"Why do I bother being polite to these people?"

A Jane Austen Mercenary appears in the distance and they are forced to hide.

Jesus, thinks Patrick, still moody in front of his television. Lux is everywhere. Every time a news report comes on he is harassing the cameraman.

Brooding, he wonders if Mike might have been fucking Lux in secret. He wouldn't put it past them. He knows that Mike is attracted to Lux, and might have won him over by agreeing to listen to some of his poetry. Lux, well known for having no morals at all, would probably do anything for a person who is willing to listen to his poetry.

Out for a drink after work, Sebastian hears from a reliable source that We Get Your Man Personnel have been making some discreet enquiries about him.

Deliriously happy, he pays for his round and rushes home to do some extra chanting.

Eugene and Grub are joined by the three remaining thrash metallists who have left some friends to guard the flat.

They gather on a corner to discuss the affair.

"We got to get the record out. What will we do if we can't find Lux and get the tape back?"

"We could record it again," suggests one of them.

"It wouldn't be as good," protests Eugene, the singer. "I could never do my vocals as well again."

"Well that wouldn't really matter," says Grub. "No one cares too much about the vocals in our sort of music. As long as I could get the lead guitar down right, we'd be OK."

Eugene is outraged. "What the fuck do you mean no one cares about the vocals? My singing makes the band."

"I wouldn't go that far," protests the drummer. "I always thought it was my powerful beat."

"Fuck your powerful beat. Any drummer can make a powerful beat. My vocals are special."

"My guitar solo was a classic."

"Your guitar solo was the same one you always play."

"It fucking well was not. I spent three days getting that guitar solo right."

"Well it just sounded the same as all the others . . ."

The argument rages for a while, as does the riot.

Johnny sees Kalia pass in the distance. He grins.

"She is never going to get back into Heaven," he says.

"Pardon, sir?" says his second-in-command.

"Nothing."

Around 45 AD Kalia is a fully qualified Hopi wise woman and can cure illnesses and find water in a drought. More importantly, by studying the behaviour of the birds in the sky, she can predict the future.

Predicting the future will be, she knows, a very useful weapon against Yasmin, who up till now has always had the upper hand.

In the tribe she is able to do hundreds of good acts, curing illness and war wounds, helping to fix tepees," staying up late to mix up body paints—all sorts of things.

Yasmin appears in the shape of a psychopathic young warrior but, now able to tell what is going to happen, Kalia starts to frustrate his evil plans.

For the third time she meets Lux, now reincarnated as a vagrant singer of traditional songs who makes his living by going round all the tribes singing to them.

74

He is not a very good singer, in fact he is terrible and the reason he wanders around is really that no one will put up with him for very long. But Kalia makes sure he gets a good meal for his singing and, knowing in advance that Yasmin is going to poison it, switches plates round the campfire so that Yasmin is poisoned instead and Lux goes away well fed.

"He was the worst singer ever to visit the tribe," says one of her friends the next day. "I think it was very kind of you to give him some bison stew."

Kalia's credit rating starts to move up again.

Lux, of course, never remembers these reincarnations. Only Kalia does. But traces of them remain in his succeeding lives. It is, for instance, the reason he knows so much poetry, having spent thousands of years learning it all over the world.

Lux seems to find himself doing a lot of hiding. Still, with police charges and violence everywhere he is probably as well to keep out of the way, being too small to be very successful at violence, also he is not very keen on it. It doesn't seem right for a poet to go around flinging bricks at people, even if they deserve it.

"Of course I could be wrong about that," he says. "After all there have been plenty of war poets. Homer maybe even fought in a war."

"What are you talking about?"

But with the cocaine still rampaging round his body, new lumps still disentangling themselves from his nose and throat to slip into his bloodstream, Lux isn't really sure what he is talking about. What he most feels like doing is going to a party or a nightclub.

"What I most feel like doing," he says to Kalia. "is going to a nightclub."

"Yuck." says Kalia. "What's this?"

It is a used condom.

"Pearl has touched that condom," says Lux. "I can sense it. I have good intuition about this sort of thing."

Lux's intuition is correct. He does have a touch of magic about him.

"Condoms can be a terrible problem. Have you ever stepped on one when you get out of bed to go to the toilet or something?"

"No."

"I have, lots of times. It is a terrible experience. It clings to your feet like a magnet. I think maybe they put glue on them so they don't accidentally come off while you're fucking. Very helpful at the time but no fun afterwards when you're groping around in the dark with sperm dribbling over your toes. Are you sure it's never happened to you?"

"No. I got bored with sex long before prophylactics were invented."

"Did you? Oh well. We must be hot on Pearl's trail now."

Lux's arms are getting a little tired from carrying his bag of possessions and his feet are sore from walking because he is wearing a threadbare pair of baseball boots that are not made for walking long distances and jumping over walls.

Inside the carrier bag he has a few clothes and a few precious possessions. One of them is a toy robot he found on a bus one time, inside a biscuit barrel. He is very very fond of this robot. Back in the high street, with the night becoming dark and a crowd of looters tearing the heavy metal shuttering off a jeweller's shop, he notices some batteries lying inside the smashed frontage of Woolworth's.

"Wait a minute, Kalia, I need a battery for my robot." He stoops down and gathers one up, thinking that if he gets it working he can cheer up Pearl with it as she is bound to be depressed after her house being burned down.

"Aha, a looter," says a policeman, and drags him off to a police van.

Up above the helicopter has switched on its spotlight and the powerful beam lights up the rooftops where the police are pursuing someone, and inside the police van the noise of the helicopter's blades is amplified so that it rings out on the metal walls and shudders around inside the young poet's head.

The noise reminds him of some time he can't quite remember and again he feels as if he is preparing to go naked into battle.

Even when Nicky used to visit Pearl and they would go to bed Pearl would always end up talking about her film. She was consumed with the creative urge.

"What it needs is something to offset all the scenes of the witches in the mansion. How about you getting me some shots from Happy Science?"

"I hate Happy Science."

"That's all right, just get a camera and take a few pictures in the laboratory of something that looks like it's evil technology and I'll cut it into my film."

Nicky agrees, if only to get Pearl off the subject and back to lovemaking.

So later she takes some pictures at random, sneaking into the science laboratories when the scientists and technicians are all over at the pub celebrating a pay rise.

Unfortunately she takes pictures of the top secret genetic programme experiments. If anyone finds out that Pearl's film is going to contain incriminating shots of illegal foetus experiments and pictures of secret computer documents, she is doomed.

"Hello? Is that We Get Your Man Personnel Limited? I am speaking on behalf of IBM. This is very secret but we are looking for a good man to take over our newly restructured European division. We have scoured the company but there is no one here that is up to it. Have you any suggestions? How about this man Flak?"

Sebastian, motivated by his inside information, is re-applying himself to his cunning scheme to have himself headhunted. Meanwhile he is getting in bad with the company directors because his work is suffering as he is too preoccupied with his machinations to do any accounting. This, however, is of little concern to him.

"I have heard that some large corporations are again expressing an interest in me," he tells Maybeline. "No doubt it is due to your advice on chanting."

Maybeline is pleased to have been of help but refuses an invitation to lunch as she already has an appointment.

Sebastian is aghast. She is having lunch with someone else. His heart aches. He resolves to chant even more to bring him success in his relationship with her.

Meanwhile he dumps the bundle of papers he is meant to be working on in a drawer, cancels an appointment with a client and shuffles off through the building to see if he can find a secretary or someone to have lunch with.

Outside the van containing the captive Lux, massed police talk over their radios, waiting for instructions about the next move.

"Personal Computer Services, let us through," says Johnny, importantly, leading his squad of elite men.

They file through Brixton.

"Do you know what's in there?" asks one of the operatives, passing the big old building that houses the Enterprise Centre.

"What?"

"Liberation Computers."

"Really?"

Johnny is interested to learn this. So this is where Liberation Computers, deadly enemies of PCS, do their subversion.

He briefly considers going in and wrecking the place but decides against it. He has a job to do.

The blessed damozel leaned out of the gold bar of Heaven, quotes Lux to himself, locked in the police van. She had three lilies in her hand and the stars in her hair were seven. I wonder if Pearl is thinking about me just now? She might even be looking for me.

AN AMBULANCE draws up and the crew try to load some of the fallen policemen into it, but it is difficult for them as the missiles keep flying and one of the ambulancemen is floored by a piece of paving stone so that he falls down right over the policeman he was trying to load onto the stretcher.

Pearl and Nicky cannot get through and they cannot go back. The crowd advances on the police and seem on the point of breaking through when round the corner a huge double file of reinforcements arrive with their shields in position and their special long riot batons at the ready. These batons were specially manufactured after the last riot to make sure the police could effectively deal with troublemakers without having to come too close.

They form up and start to advance. Trained for this sort of thing, they force the rioters back. Snatch squads appear from among their ranks, targeting particular people for arrest and dragging them off face down with their arms pinned behind their backs.

They have been well trained. Funds have been diverted from other places to strengthen the police and prepare them for riots. So now the government can deal with riots without having to come too close.

Beside Pearl a young woman is poleaxed by a constable, and the crowd, sensing they are about to be overwhelmed, start to panic and everbody tries to escape.

Pearl tries to grab Nicky but Nicky panics along with the crowd and struggles away. A snatch squad comes between them and they are separated.

Lux is sitting in the police van waiting to be charged with looting a nine-volt battery, but he is not too worried. For one thing he is too stoned to worry much and for another he never lets anything trouble him, save for his painful love affair.

This optimism is soundly rooted.

"My optimism is soundly rooted," he exclaims out of the blue to the man sitting next to him in the van. "When I was six years years old I fell underneath a lawnmower my dad was testing for the company. It could've been a terrible disaster. It could've left me so mangled and disfigured I'd be ashamed to walk the streets. But all that happened was it gave me this little scar over my eye. I kinda like it. Sort of pirate-like, don't you think?"

He gets no reply. But if even falling under a prototype lawnmower turned out well he is sure that nothing really bad can happen to him. And, so far, all his life he has enjoyed the luck and protection of the truly innocent, and every time he is thrown out of a squat he finds a new one quickly enough, or someone attracted by his looks puts him up for a while, and when he spends all his Giro an hour after he gets it on drugs, robots, and carrier bags then someone looks after him for the next fortnight or he finds twenty pence on the street and twenty pence is enough to live on for a day if you can manage on a bar of chocolate, which Lux can.

Sometimes the people he is looked after by get fed up with him thieving everything and spending hours in front of the mirror doing his hair and make-up and sometimes he gets bored and leaves, because he is never really able to merge his life with anyone else's.

"Mind you," he continues. "I never really trusted my father after that. It was rumoured in the family that he pushed me deliberately."

Even inside the police van the air smells of burning.

"The prolonged candle flames flung their smoke into the laquearia," he says out loud. "That's T.S. Eliot." The line sort of sticks in his mind because he has no idea what a laquearia is. Possibly it is something you spray on hair lacquer with.

"Shut up," grunts another of the van's occupants, having a cracked rib and not being in the mood to hear any poetry or stories of Lux's childhood.

Lux takes out his crayon and starts to write on the side of the van, making up a poem as he goes along.

The Jane Austen Mercenaries continue their search although they have had a furious argument about who is the most important member of the band and are now barely speaking to each other. This makes it difficult for them to agree on which street to look in next and with the police everywhere shoving people about and some streets impassable with burning debris it is proving to be a difficult task.

"Where now?" rasps Eugene.

"Don't ask me," says the drummer. "I am just a worthless accessory. According to you anyone can keep a beat. If you're so smart, you find him."

Nicky runs off and hides in a council estate behind a rubbish skip and Pearl can't find her.

Alone except for the colonies of insects that make a good living hunting through the rubbish left by the refuse truck, Nicky lies quietly, unable to move.

Her psychosis is getting worse and worse as she becomes more and more guilty about killing the computer. As a master programmer she had her own little computer on her desk. When she thinks about how she set fire to it and threw it through a window she hates herself. After all it wasn't the computer's fault that she had such a bad time at Happy Science.

She imagines it lying in a grave somewhere, cold and unloved, circuits dead and casing all rusted. Worse, she imagines Personal Computer Services coming and taking her away and putting her in a secret prison where no one will ever find her.

To make it even more frightening, no one else but her believes in the computer police; they think she is just being paranoid when she talks about them. Even Pearl does not really believe in them.

"Hello, Personal Computer Services?" Dr. Carlson is on the phone. "Any progress yet? No?"

"Fraid not," they tell him. "We haven't been able to find her yet."

"Well this is not very satisfactory. This woman has committed one of the major anti-computer crimes of the century, you know, wrecking the machine and making off with the programme. It is time you did something about it."

They tell him to be patient. They always get results.

The Chairman happens by and asks him how things are progressing.

"Not well. We are stuck without the genetic data in the programme. I could kill that woman. And Socrates wants more and more publicity. The man is practically insane."

The chairman tries to calm him down. He knows that the Doctor no longer gets on with anyone.

Kalia watches Lux being hauled off into the police van. Unable to do anything about it, she continues on her way, doing what acts of kindness she can.

The riot is making little impression on her. Having lived hundreds of lives, she has seen hundreds of riots.

The twentieth century has made an impression on her. She doesn't like it. Particularly she doesn't like where she has to live, a bedsit in Camberwell. The bedsit is terrible. She has been more comfortable sleeping in a swamp with a wolfskin for a blanket. Thousands of years after being exiled from Heaven she still finds her surroundings hard to take and has never forgotten the luxury of her heavenly life.

Earlier that day a starling had flown past her window.

That is interesting, she thinks. There is going to be a riot.

Furthermore, the birds tell her that somewhere in the riot a direct descendant of the Queen of Heaven will be endangered.

She thinks that she must now be close to her tally of one million kind acts. Completely worn out by it all, she hopes she is, but she lost track somewhere around the sixteenth century, when she was an Inca and the Spaniards invaded South America. If I rescue this descendant of the Queen of Heaven from danger it might be the very thing that gets me reinstated, she muses.

So far in this lifetime she has not encountered the evil Yasmin.

Gerry and his friend Mark wander the streets, looking at the riot without participating. Gerry takes mental notes for the article he is going to write for *Uptown*.

In a crowd they run into Sheila, a friend from the days when Gerry was big in his student union.

Discussing the riot, they are both enthusiastic.

"I met someone you know, a little while ago."

"Who?"

"Nicky. Do you know she has a manuscript of Mary Luxembourg's new novel?"

Gerry frowns.

"She had. It was burned."

"No, I met her and another girl a while ago and she still had it. I held it while we hunted in the bag for some cigarettes."

"Quick," yells Gerry to Mark, "I must find a phone."

They struggle out of the crowd to look for a phone but it is not easy, hardly any phones work in Brixton at the best of times and now most of them are either freshly wrecked or unreachable.

I can't let that retrospective go out if the book still exists, thinks Gerry, worried.

Back in twelfth-century Japan the perfume-guessing contest is under way with Lux and two brothers from the family on one side and three important locals from the next hamlet on the other, including the man with the god-given nose.

Kalia's heart sinks when they arrive. Another of the important locals is Yasmin. With her growing ability to read the future she has been expecting this, but in the rigidly hierarchical society of ancient Japan it is difficult for her to avoid him. As usual Yasmin has been reincarnated in the more important position. While Kalia is youngest daughter and someone to be married off as quickly as possible, Yasmin is lord of his hamlet.

He lets loose a malevolent grin. By now both Yasmin and Kalia can easily recognise each other's spirits whatever bodies they are inhabiting at the time. As Kalia brings out some tea for everyone, Yasmin cunningly trips her up, just to keep his eye in, and the tea spills everywhere, ruining Lux's new kimono.

Lux is practically in tears as he has spent hours in front of a mirror arranging his clothes till they are perfect and it takes all of Kalia's skill to calm him down. He makes such a fuss about his kimono that if it were not for the fact that it would set her back in her task such a long way she would have strangled him with it.

11

GET A GRIP, Nicky tells herself. Stop being so appalled at everything. The world may not be so bad.

While she hides under the skip seven men with knives drag a young woman into the entance of the flats to rape her, removing her clothes and taking turns to make her do what they want.

While one has his turn the others look on and make comments and pass round a can of beer.

Nicky is too scared to help the victim and there is nowhere to run for help.

The woman trembles with sick terror and does what the men want so as not to be killed.

Above her eyes the rapist's face looms huge and wet with folds of skin hanging down, filling with excited blood.

"How d'you like that, bitch."

"Keep her legs open."

"You do it good or I'll cut your face into bits."

"Yes," says Gerry, further up the road, as missiles still fly and fighting rages. "It is very true that a riot is the voice of the unheard."

"Hi," he says, meeting Eugene on the fringes of a large crowd which is shuffling unwillingly up the street, directed and occasionally prodded by a line of policemen.

Knowing each other slightly they talk and Gerry hears about Lux stealing the tape.

"Can't you record it again?" he suggests, but all this suggestion gets is some angry silence from the other members of the band.

"How about I take some pictures of you in the riot?" asks Mark, brandishing his camera. "Be great publicity material for the single. If you get it out."

"We're busy looking for Lux," says Eugene.

"It'll be good publicity. Let's do the pictures," says Grub, keen to disagree with the singer.

"I wanna be in the front of the photo this time," says the drummer. "I'm fed up with being obscured by everyone else."

"It's my turn to be in the front," complains the bass guitarist.

"What the fuck are you doing?" demands the large body next to Lux.

"Writing a poem," he explains.

"Well fucking stop it."

Lux stops, not wanting to be harassed in the confined space of the police van.

The door rattles.

"Take this," says the man next to Lux, and stuffs something into his hand.

It is three diamond rings and a packet of something. The door swings open and some police look in.

Lux crams the looted rings and the packet into his mouth.

A policeman drags him out of the van.

"What you got, sonny?"

"Mmmbgmm," replies Lux, trying desperately to keep the rings hidden without swallowing them. He knows that it will be bad for his insides if he does.

The policeman looks in his bag. Seeing the toy robot, spare army trousers, and Star Wars toothbrush he realises that Lux is not a very dangerous character and they need the space in the van for a very dangerous character they have just arrested.

"I caught him nicking a battery," explains the arresting officer.

The packet Lux is hiding contains more cocaine and the paper starts to come apart in Lux's mouth, freezing his tongue till he can hardly feel the rings any more. I'm doomed, he thinks. I'll get thrown in prison as a drug dealer and looter and I'll never see Pearl again.

"What the fuck have you got on your hair?" says the sergeant to Lux. "Piss off out of here. If I see you again, you're nicked." And he gives Lux a shove. Lux scurries off and round a corner.

He spits out the rings but there is not much of the cocaine left to spit out and on top of his earlier dose Lux feels like he is walking somewhere between the clouds and Alpha Centauri.

Another stroke of luck, he muses. Let out of the police van with a free mouthful of cocaine. I must have had ounces of the stuff tonight and normally I can't even afford to buy a little line. He does stay firmly enough in reality to notice members of the Jane Austen Mercenaries lurking on the next corner and to hurry off in the opposite direction. He wonders what he should do with all the demo tapes. Possibly he could record some of his poetry on them and send it to radio stations. That seems like a good idea.

Regarding diamond rings as hopelessly tacky he throws them into a garden and starts trying to work his way round the now heavily police-fortified centre of Brixton.

He makes it through an estate and down towards Stockwell where he is jostled by some men with beercans.

Strange dreams filter into his mind. They frequently do. For some reason he finds himself thinking of bison stew, although as far as he knows he has never eaten a bison. In fact he would hate to eat a bison.

Some youths stand next to him. "Nice night," says Lux, politely. Two of them take hold of his arms and hold him while another searches him. Finding no money, they go away.

"I've just been searched. I'm meant to be searching for Pearl. Where is she? What the fuck were those people mugging me for? Do I look like I've got any money?" He talks out loud to himself, unable to hear his thoughts too well above the wailing of sirens and stamping angry feet.

"Lux, involved in one of history's great love affairs, scours the violent streets for Pearl Freedom Fighter. Refusing offer after offer to stop and read poems to television cameras he sticks single-mindedly to his task."

Perhaps it wasn't such a good idea to get obsessed in a love affair. On the other hand it is probably necessary for a young poet. No doubt Milton never had a moment's peace from having affairs all the time. Lux, utterly determined now to find Pearl, resolves to let nothing stand in his path and marches on resolutely.

Sebastian is now chanting furiously, spending much more time on it than Maybeline's suggested fifteen minutes each day.

He is completely determined to have himself headhunted.

Also, he is completely determined to win Maybeline's heart, but he suspects that she may be starting some relationship with a successful public relations expert from the company next door.

He has heard more rumours that Ace and We Get Your Man have been continuing their discreet enquiries about him and now completely believes in the power of the mantra.

This, along with phone calls to Maybeline and careful study of mercenary magazines, takes up all his time so he is unable to do any accounting for Happy Science, but this is nothing to worry about for a man with a bright future as head of Coca Cola or General Motors.

Kalia lives through more lifetimes struggling with the world's evil, and with Yasmin.

She scores a notable success when she finds herself in the middle of a plague in fifth-century Nigeria and helps tend thousands of victims.

Whenever Yasmin comes near she is now able to predict his whereabouts and move on. Having lived for so long on Earth she has also picked up a fair amount of expertise in physical violence, always useful for defending your peasant community; but she never thinks of fighting with Yasmin because it would only count as a bad deed and deduct from her total. She is fighting an unfair battle but carries on determinedly. The plague is very widespread and there are victims for her to minister to everywhere.

In her next life, as a peasant in Peru, she has a hard time just staying alive. But soon after, whatever god is unfairly rigging her incarnations lets his attention slip for a moment and she is born as Queen Guinevere. Of course her life ends fairly sadly but while she is King Arthur's wife she does kindnesses by the score, always helping knights out with their problems and feeding the poor round the castle.

A wandering minstrel appears. It is Lux, dressed in colourful rags and carrying a lute. He asks permission to play the Knights of the Round Table a few songs and, since they are all hopelessly drunk after a day's jousting, he goes down reasonably well.

Staying in the castle he falls in love with a young princess, another in the endless series of impossible love affairs that Lux gets tangled up in through the ages.

Kalia does her best to help by way of introductions and message-carrying, but it is a hopeless proposition because the princess is not a music or poetry fan and Lux can't do anything else. Finally he is banished after being caught trying to climb a creeper into her bedroom.

Before being banished he pleads eloquently to King Arthur for clemency, saying that it was an affair of the heart and he was overcome by his passions, but when Sir Galahad, always a sneak, points out that it was in fact the wrong bedroom Lux was trying to climb into King Arthur gets the impression that possibly Lux is not too fussy which young princess he crawls into bed with, and tells him to leave the kingdom.

Kalia, as Guinevere, dies being regarded as a saint. She nearly always does. People are astonished at her tireless energy in doing good. Mind you, she is actually totally sick of it. Sometimes she feels like poisoning a well or massacring a few hundred innocents, but this, of course, will not get her back into Heaven.

Nicky is in shock. Already racked with guilt for killing her computer, the sight of the rape has pushed her into deep trauma.

Pearl hunts the area for her, hampered by prowling police cars that drive round the blocks and over the grass verges like panthers.

Finally she notices a familiar shoe.

"Nicky, come on, get out from behind that skip."

Nicky lets herself be led out but doesn't say anything and her face stands out white in the night. Pearl, grasping Nicky and her film, hustles her along, feeling like she has been hustling them along for hours without making any progress, just as she has been making the film for months without making progress, just like everything else winding its way along, never coming to a satisfactory end.

Gerry eventually finds a phone outside the police station. The police are letting the press use it and he has a press card.

"Cancel the Mary Luxembourg retrospective," he tells the magazine. "There has been a major re-evaluation of her in critical circles."

"But you only phoned up an hour ago."

"Things move fast in the literary world."

"Are you going to give us a report on the riot?"

"Shortly. Right now I am busy gathering exclusive material." He puts the phone down and it is eagerly wrestled over by waiting pressmen. He goes back to where Mark is photographing the Jane Austen Mercenaries.

"That's right," says Mark. "Scowl."

"Right Mark, we've got to find the manuscript."

Now it exists and is recoverable, Gerry is once again in line for plaudits from Mary Luxembourg. Things are looking up, as long as he finds Nicky.

Personal Computer Services have not found it easy looking for Nicky because she has left few clues as to her whereabouts. Johnny does eventually track her to Pearl's house, but before he can do anything the riot starts and he loses them when the house burns down. Johnny is becoming increasingly mad about everything. He is just waiting for somebody to attack him and when they do then he is going to kill them.

Lux, previously indifferent to the riot, is starting to get a little fed up with it. It is keeping him from Pearl. If he doesn't see Pearl regularly he gets withdrawal symptoms.

"It's not, as I thought, that death creates love. More that love knows death."

Walking on, Lux passes, in the space of one block of flats, from an area of calm to one of violent activity, where some policemen are struggling and fighting their way through heavy resistance to try and clear the estate of rioters, some of whom are up on the balconies throwing petrol bombs. Temporarily distracted, he forgets to look where he is going and bumps into a press photographer.

How fortuitous, thinks Lux.

"Take my picture?" he asks, polite as ever. The photographer ignores him, so Lux stands in front of the camera.

"Get out of the fucking way, kid," says the photographer, hardened to troublesome onlookers.

"Why won't you take my picture? What's the matter, isn't my hair looking good?" He hunts around for his hand mirror.

By the children's play area a policeman with a bleeding face is wrestling with a man with a knife and five other policemen pile in. The photographer is trying for some action shots but Lux is persistent. "I'm a local poet. I edit a music paper. I play in a thrash metal band. I'm a cult figure. Get me in your newspaper. Tell them to send down their literary editor for a few words."

This sort of storytelling is nothing to Lux who one time phoned up the BBC World Service to ask if he could host their arts roundup programme.

"I'm here to photograph the riot."

"I am a rioter. I've been rioting all evening. I'm just having a break."

Finally the photographer is forced to move away and misses his action shots, although as what is happening now is the police are breaking the arm of the man with the knife, his editor wouldn't have printed them anyway.

Damn photographers, thinks Lux, outraged at not being photo'd when he is a lot better looking than any of the policemen around. Photographers should be tied up in sacks and drowned.

"You wouldn't know a good picture if it poked you in the eye!" he shouts after the departing pressman.

"No wonder your paper is rubbish! Remember to mention me to the literary editor."

"Lux!"

Hmm, thinks Lux, figures stampeding towards him. I'd forgotten all about the Jane Austen Mercenaries. He sprints off, looking for a wall to climb.

Pearl and Nicky, resting, are moved on by a policeman who suggests loudly to his colleague that they are whores waiting for niggers off the estate, a good and clever insult.

"No wonder the whole place is going up in smoke," screams Pearl, and gets a violent push for her trouble.

Foolishly, she pushes back, which is enough to have her arrested and jailed by a magistrate for assaulting an officer, or maybe actual bodily harm if the officer is looking for some more serious offences to bolster up his arrest sheet.

A delicate position is reached where the officer ponders briefly whether or not to make the arrest. He is temporarily disadvantaged by Lux, scrambling blindly over a wall and landing on his head.

"Pearl!" he yells, delighted. "I've found you."

"You're all nicked," gasps the policeman, disentangling himself from Lux and looking round for support. His patrol, however, is just now coming under heavy fire from a rooftop and cannot come to his aid, and his sergeant shouts for him to come and help.

Undecided, the policeman hesitates.

"Stop hanging around like a fool, Lux," says Kalia, appearing over the wall.

She drags him away, followed by Pearl and Nicky, to some temporary refuge up on another, quieter balcony.

The police, having now broken up the fierce resistance around the estate, are picking up everyone they can fit into their vans.

There seems to be nowhere to go for safety.

Mr. Socrates of the publicity department is, after the Chairman and Managing Director, the most powerful man in Happy Science. He is suspicious of Sebastian Flak. He does not know quite what is going on but he thinks that something is.

Sebastian is inducing suspicion of himself by continually making phone calls and slamming down the phone if anyone else enters the room. Or else he disappears from his office for long periods.

What he is doing when he disappears, though, is reading *Soldier of Fortune* or chanting, something he now does in the executive toilet.

Maybeline seems more willing to meet him for lunch these days.

LUX, KALIA, PEARL, AND NICKY find a landing in the block of flats that is relatively free from urine, dog shit, and rubbish that spews out from the hopelessly inadequate garbage disposal chutes. They settle down for a rest. Down below some rioting is still going on.

"Pearl," says Lux, gripping her arm, overcome with emotion and finding it difficult to speak.

"Hello Lux," says Pearl, prising loose his fingers and making some comment about limpets. Lux's voice returns.

"I've been looking all over for you. I was worried you might have been burned to death in the fire or killed in the riot or arrested."

"You just about got us arrested, falling all over that policeman."

"I saved you."

"No you didn't, we were leaving safely when you almost ruined it." Lux ignores this.

"I've written you a new poem." He scrabbles round in his carrier bag looking for the piece of paper with the poem on it.

Pearl is intent on comforting Nicky, who is staring out into space, wild and deranged, but Lux is too insistent in his passion to notice anything like this and rambles on and on about what he has been doing that night and how many poems he has read to televsion cameras and

97

how he has told some important media people all about Pearl's film so she can be famous as well as him and sits so close to Pearl that he is practically on top of her and asks her what she is doing tonight and would she like to pay him into a nightclub if she has any spare money because his hair is looking particuarly good with his new KY jelly and sugar setting gel and he figures he should show it off to the public, forgetting that what they are all doing is hiding from a riot.

"Be quiet, Lux," she says, eventually.

Lux smiles at her, his best smile, capable of melting the most unfriendly heart.

"You've been practising your smile in front of the mirror again," she says.

Lux looks hurt. He starts to sniffle.

"Don't bother," says Pearl. "I know you practise crying as well."

"She is horrible to me," complains Lux to Kalia, but immediately turns back to Pearl, not really insulted because he knows that deep inside Pearl is crazy about him.

"Did I introduce you to Kalia? She has been exiled from Heaven for three-thousand years."

"Lux, have you been fucking someone for cocaine again?"

"The last lot of photos were shit," moans the drummer to his fellow Mercenaries. "You couldn't hardly see me at all. I got fans too, you know."

"Stop whining about the damn photos," says Grub. "We still got to find Lux."

"I'm going to kill him."

"Me too."

"And me."

"And me. I just don't wanna be obscured in the photos again."

"Where we gonna look now?"

There doesn't seem any logical way of searching so they just carry on walking the streets.

With the twelfth-century Japanese incarnation of Lux on their side, the Yamamoto family massacre the opposition in the first round of the contest. Sake flows freely in the victory celebration.

"Chang Kwai Lux," says Lord Yamamoto, "you were sensational. All the most obscure perfumes from the far-flung corners of the world and you named every one, no trouble. The whole town is proud of you."

Lux, completely wrecked on sake, accepts the thanks graciously and carries on composing a poem he is writing to the eldest daughter of the household, with whom he is smitten. She is pledged to be married to the Emperor's nephew but this does not worry Lux overmuch as he has heard that the Emperor's nephew is a dolt who spends all his time practising swordplay and planning to invade China. No doubt Lux will be able to win her heart.

Kalia congratulates him later.

"You finally did something successfully after a thousand years of trying," she tells him.

"Yes, the contest did seem to take a thousand years," replies Lux, not understanding what she means.

"Will you take this poem to Shimono for me? Stuff it under her door tonight and tomorrow tell her it's from a secret admirer. Insinuate the admirer is me but don't come right out with it."

"It will come to no good."

Lux shrugs.

In the guest room the beaten opponents are furious, particularly Lord Yasmin. He plots something for the following day. No one is going to humiliate his perfume-guessing team.

Sebastian's day starts off well when he puts on an Australian accent and phones Ace Headhunters on behalf of Rio Tinto Zinc to ask if they have any information on the talented accountant Sebastian Flak and Ace Headhunters say they are at that moment trying to contact him, but it worsens with a troubling experience while he is quietly chanting in the executive toilet.

A vision of Lux floats into his head. He sees the small ragged figure again standing outside the Happy Science building trying to persuade people that he is a genius. This vision worries him because he is still attracted to the figure. Worse, Sebastian starts being carried back in time so that he imagines himself as a knight in a castle somewhere, and Lux is still hanging around, playing a lute and causing general distress.

Unhappy about having visions thrust upon him when all he wants is a powerful position somewhere and no problems, Sebastian wonders if he should stop his chanting for a while because, after all, success seems to be headed his way already.

But he needs to carry on. He believes it is helping him with Maybeline. If he stops he might lose out to the public relations expert in the company next door. Sebastian has started to hate public relations experts. When Mr. Socrates comes around he no longer speaks to him.

With Lux monopolising Pearl, Kalia, noticing that Nicky is in a bad way, draws her into a conversation. Normally this would not be possible for anyone except Pearl as Nicky is now appalled at the whole world, but Kalia, three thousand years of kindness behind her, is capable of most things.

Nicky starts to tell her about her grim experiences at Happy Science.

"As a compromise between the scientific laboratories and the publicity department Dr. Carlson told me I had to enter the beauty contest and be mother to some genius babies. When I asked why me he said I was clever and quite nice-looking. Mr. Socrates thought I wouldn't look too bad on television although he would still have preferred a professional model."

"What did you do?" asks Kalia, deeply sympathetic.

"I refused. I told them it was stupid and degrading. Then Dr. Carlson said he would sack me if I didn't."

"And then?"

"I had a nervous breakdown, killed my computer, stole the genetic programme, and fled."

She buries her face in her hands. Her hands are filthy from hiding behind the skip.

"Well," says Mr. Socrates, later, "I told you we should have got a professional model. We'll just have to hope this doesn't reach the papers."

"My genetic programme is gone," mumbles Dr. Carlson, ashen. "The work is ruined. I was to be nominated for a Nobel prize . . ."

"Well can't you just get another copy?"

"No. She wiped them all. Fifteen year's work, all gone."

"Don't worry. I'll get Personal Computer Services onto her. They won't muck about. What about the new toothpaste?"

Lux is holding Pearl's hand. This is enough to make him happy. Content with the world, he stops talking. Pearl, still holding her film, is relieved that it is still in existence. Nicky, comforted by Kalia, seems a little less manic.

For a while, peace reigns.

Mr. Socrates suspects that Sebastian has had something to do with the theft of the genetic programme because he has noticed how disloyal to the company he has become. He starts keeping an eye on him and taps his phone calls and so learns that some big headhunting operation is under way.

That's odd, he thinks. Why would General Motors be interested in Sebastian Flak? Everyone knows he is no good for anything. Also he hears Sebastian on the phone to Maybeline, talking about chanting. He finds this very suspicious and assumes that he is talking to an American accomplice in code.

It seems like further proof that the accountant had a hand in the theft. Perhaps he is bribing a new company to take him by supplying them with stolen details of the research.

He has him carefully watched.

Patrick, watching television, sees Mike approaching and entering the Enterprise Centre, an old department store recently converted.

"Damn Liberation Computers," he mutters. He blames them for taking up all of Mike's time. They are as much to blame for the rift in their relationship as the awful Lux.

Lying with a Friend under a Burnt-out Truck

"Is the riot still going on?"

"I think so."

"It's quite peaceful under this truck. Look, there's a beetle. I quite like beetles. I squatted in a basement with some beetles. Several times. They are much misunderstood. So am I. Did I ever tell you about my parents throwing me out of the house?"

"Yes Lux."

"It was the day after they caught me in bed with my sister. I got flung out with a plastic bag full of clothes and twenty pence I'd stolen from the telephone box. A bit harsh, I always thought. It was only my second offence. Well, only the second one they could prove. I always got blamed for everything. My father used to say no one with any morals ever came out of a test tube."

"What happened to your sister?"

"She went to work on an oil rig. She was pretty tough. I never hear from her any more."

There is a small, sad pause.

"I remember when I had to go naked into battle. It was in the Trojan War. I got sent out with a sword and a shield and nothing else."

"Lux, you're rambling."

"No I'm not. It's true. I got killed. A man is supple and weak when living, but hard and stiff when dead, as Lao Tzu said. I feel funny."

SEBASTIAN'S EFFORTS at marketing himself, given strength by the huge amounts of psychic energy he was putting into them, begin to show some powerful results.

Happy Science starts to crawl with operatives from all London's headhunting companies, each of them trying to organise a secret meeting with the now sought-after accountant.

Disguised as window cleaners and firms of healthy-sandwich makers they trample the carpeted corridors of the executive block with contracts bulging in their pockets, all eager to get hold of the man who is fast becoming the sensation of the business world.

Furthermore, managing directors around the country, hearing rumours at their golfing clubs, start thinking that if Sebastian Flak is getting all this attention then he really must be hot property.

"IBM is on the point of stealing one of the country's leading executives," they say to their subordinates. "Why have we made no attempt to secure the services of this man?" So genuine enquiries start being made and the whole process escalates till it becomes the most talked-about business in the City.

Sebastian, however, keen to push up his market value, spends most of his time reading *Soldier of Fortune* in the toilet, holding out against accepting an offer too soon, although when he mentions to Maybeline at lunch that everyone is after him to offer him a new job she is of the opinion that he should get on and take one, because Maybeline is a practical sort of person. Always keen to take her advice, Sebastian arranges a meeting.

Over the main course Maybeline tells him how much she admires Britain's new determination to go with the free market economy and over dessert she mentions how much she dislikes homosexuals. Brought up in a conservative family she finds them disgusting.

"Would you like to spend another day in the country with me?" asks Lux, on the landing with the others.

"No," replies Pearl.

"Why not?"

"Because last time you tried riding on a sheep and I had to bandage your ankle and help you to the bus stop. And before that you insisted on going into that barn and bawling out your poem about having sex with sharks. I've never had to run so fast in my life."

"No," admits Lux. "Faced with forty panicstricken cows we didn't have much choice. But I enjoyed it."

Pearl gives him an evil look.

"It is quiet down below," says Kalia. "I have a friend who lives a few blocks away. If we go there she will make us some tea."

Everyone is dying for a cup of tea, so they set off.

Johnny receives a call from Mr. Socrates on his portable phone. He reports that so far they have had no positive results, despite sighting their quarry. It proved impossible to keep track of her in the chaos of rioting, police cars, and fire engines.

"Is there any sign of Sebastian Flak down there?"

"No. Should there be?"

"Possibly. I intercepted a call to his office. He has arranged a meeting with Coca Cola somewhere in the vicinity, presumably thinking it would be an unobtrusive spot for a rendezvous. Now he's in the thick of a riot. Keep your eyes open, you know we suspect him of being mixed up in this whole business."

"Right," says Johnny.

He likes his work. He likes tracking people down and having them arrested. He likes doing anything that will frustrate people's dreams. He always has, in every life.

He is Yasmin, and dreadfully evil.

Walking through the now empty courtyards, Pearl holds Nicky's hand to comfort her. Lux becomes dimly aware that he is not number one in Pearl's affections.

Momentarily sad, he remembers that Pearl is only being kind to Nicky, who is of course a candidate for an asylum. An understanding sort of person, Lux can accept this. No doubt Pearl will soon have more time for him.

He is warmly glowing from his gigantic dose of cocaine, slightly bleeding from his head, and still clutching his carrier bag full of possessions. As is Pearl. While Lux has his Star Wars toothbrush and spare army trousers, she has her film.

"I left my cap behind when I was evicted," announces Lux, for no apparent reason. "I miss it terribly. I used to look good in it, in fact I looked sensational. It used to stop traffic. People sometimes came up to me in the street and said what a nice hat it was. It was brilliant. It was the world's best hat. I used to look sensational in it. People in clubs used to stop me and ask where I got it. My hat was—"

"Lux"

"—a masterpiece of headwear. It used to set off my hair to perfection. I used to organise my make-up around it. One time a woman stopped me in the street and wanted to take my picture. She said that my features were striking, and so was the hat. She said—"

"Lux, will you shut up about your damn hat?" says Pearl.

Lux manages to stay silent for a few seconds.

"Jane Russell wore a hat quite like it in a film one time," he says, defiantly.

The riot being a flexible thing, it suddenly reappears as they reach the main road.

Used to it by now, none of them reacts much as a crowd of rioters flee round a corner towards them, pursued by the police, because they are all looking forward to a nice cup of tea and not much concerned with anything else, but as well as being engulfed by more fighting they are suddenly engulfed by a fire engine which mounts the pavement out of control and explodes in flames all around them, creating terrible confusion. The police and rioters pause briefly to wonder if they should carry on fighting or run away from the explosion or help the crew or throw stones at them or just stand by and watch. Standing by to watch, Lux, Kalia, Pearl, and Nicky are engulfed by a further explosion which renders Lux unconscious.

"Well," says the Chairman to Dr. Carlson, "it's all very well you complaining to me about the publicity department ruining your project but from what I understand it was your fault that the genetic programme went missing. Apparently the woman who stole it was your selection for the mothers' contest."

This is true. Dr. Carlson shifts around uncomfortably.

"And I understand she caused a considerable amount of damage. Very bad for our image, one of our employees doing a thing like that. Do we have any idea why she did it?"

"Only the note she left."

"What did it say?"

The Doctor pulls a copy out from his well-worn lab coat. It is his lucky lab coat. He has resolved never to change it until he wins a Nobel Prize.

Dear Happy Science Scumbags,
      I am sick to death of your ridiculous fascist artificial breed-
ing programme. I am sick to death of your utterly insulting and
oppressive competition to find a suitable mother for the genius
babies. I am disgusted at Dr. Carlson trying to make me, a prize-
winning biologist, enter the competition. I am sick of not being
able to walk along the corridor without some fucking moron staring at my tits or commenting on my legs. I hate you all. I have
pictures of your illegal genetic experiments which will shortly be
appearing in a film. I intend to destroy the project and hope the
company goes bankrupt.

This was not the cleverest thing that Nicky could have done, giving
her hand away. But, already upset by the sight of her computer plunging eight storeys to a terrible death, she was not thinking clearly at the
time.

"The ravings of a madwoman."

Along the corridor Sebastian reels out of the executive toilet. He has
just had a terrible experience while chanting, a powerful and sustained
vision of himself as a rich landowner in eighteenth-century Scotland,
turning peasants off the land to make way for sheep. The sheep would
make money and the peasants could do what they liked, which was
mainly to starve.

LUX DREAMS AGAIN of going into a battle with only a sword and a shield and then dreams of being in Heaven but when he wakes up in a bathroom with two-tone fleck paint on the walls he knows he is not in Heaven but in a hard-to-let council flat in Lambeth because all hard-to-let council flats in Lambeth have two-tone fleck on the bathroom walls, and in the kitchen.

Kalia is dabbing his head with a cloth.

"Careful with my make-up," says Lux, slightly weak. "What happened?"

"You got knocked out by an exploding fire engine."

"Where's Pearl?"

"She went to hospital with Nicky in an ambulance. They got hit by debris. They'll be all right."

Lux leaps to his feet, howling. It is almost too much to bear. He has found the love of his life only to see her kidnapped by a doctor.

"What's wrong with these people?" he demands. "Don't they have any sensitivity at all? You hunt for hours in a riot looking for your girlfriend and first thing they do is throw her in an ambulance. I've got to find her."

Kalia pushes him back in the chair.

"You should rest. You've been unconscious twice tonight."

"I feel alright. But depressed. Pearl's been stolen. Why didn't you put me in the ambulance with her?"

"I was too busy hiding you under a bush from an irate bunch of musicians."

"Oh."

Lux looks glum. Pearl has been stolen.

"I just can't stand it," he says sincerely.

"Cheer up," says Kalia kindly. "After all, at least you know Pearl is safe now. And she'll just stay in the hospital till the riot is over and then you can go and visit her."

Lux brightens up.

"That's true. She is bound to stay there with Nicky. Did you notice what a sicko Nicky is? I am as sympathetic as anyone to sickos, in fact probably more so, but Pearl would be a lot better off with me. When she was getting carried into the ambulance did she call my name?"

"No."

"Are you sure?"

"Yes."

"Maybe just muttered it softly?"

"No."

"Maybe there is something wrong with your hearing. Or possibly you couldn't make it out over the riot. Anyway, she was probably thinking it." Optimism floods into him. "Did you notice how keen she was to hold my hand? Just about mangled my fingers. And we arranged a day in the country. In fact this has not been a bad night, I got to hold hands with Pearl and I got stuffed full of cocaine."

"You got thrown out of your home."

"I'll find another one."

"You got hit with a brick and mugged."

"It happens."

Lux sniffs, nose still congested.

"Why do you take drugs?"

"Why not?"

"Well that's as good a logical answer as I've heard in three thousand years."

In the entrance hall of the Enterprise Centre, newsman after newsman dictates reports about valiant police battling against bestial black rioters.

Outside, a TV crew is interviewing a young black woman.

"I've been for thirty-two interviews and can't get a job," she tells them.

The winter in Gdansk in 1792 is particularly harsh and everywhere children and the elderly are dying, succumbing helplessly to the elements that bite through their clothes and eat away their bones.

It is bitterly cold and the frozen poor huddle pathetically in their slums without firewood for heat or food for sustenance. "What do you want?" demands a rich moneylender, annoyed at being called away from his blazing, roaring, forest-consuming fire by a woman garbed as a nun but much too insistent for his liking.

"The water comes through the roof of my flat and the council haven't got anyone to fix the water tank upstairs so the walls are all damp and the baby's sick," says the woman, continuing the interview. "I got struck off the social security because I was three minutes late for my re-start interview and it took five weeks to get my benefit sorted out."

"I'd like a little more time for the families round my abbey to pay you back," says the nun. "They have no money for food or firewood."

"Well, they should have thought of that before they borrowed money off me," replies Sebastian, who is the moneylender, motioning for one of his servants to show her the door.

"And tell them if they don't meet the payments I'll repossess their houses."

"It could lead to trouble."

"Then they will all be thrown in jail."

"I go out to a social club once a month and last time I was there the police came in and separated all the blacks from the whites and searched the blacks."

"Is this any reason to riot?" asks the reporter.

The woman shrugs and goes away to try and reclaim her baby from the babysitter somewhere across town.

The interview is shown on television but along with all the other reports it soon becomes either lost or meaningless, not being dramatic enough to grab anyone's attention.

The nun leaves. The moneylender settles down to some wine. Sebastian comes back to his senses with a sudden jolt, finding himself in the executive toilet. Outside his cubicle he can hear some directors discussing last night's football.

"Another one," he mutters. "I'm getting fed up with these visions of past lives. I don't even believe in past lives. What is causing them? And why am I always so horrible in them? At least that brat with the yellow hair wasn't in this one."

Really he knows what is causing them. It is the religious chanting causing disruptions in his psyche. His psyche, previously concerned only with being rich and powerful, cannot cope with this new burst of spiritualism.

However, he cannot give it up because of the success it is bringing him. And Maybeline wouldn't like it.

"There is something wrong," says Lux. "Everyone is rioting."

"Very astute, Lux," says Kalia. "Now keep still while I bandage your head."

Pearl, knocked unconscious by the exploding fire engine and Nicky, uninjured but comatose, moan, struggle, and dream of each other as the ambulance crawls its way through the chaos to the hospital.

"Do you think I should be out rioting?" muses Lux.

"I don't think you'd fit in too well."

Lux quotes Kalia the four lines he made up in the police van and then makes up a second verse.

"Very nice," says Kalia, still bandaging his head. "What does it mean?"

"I haven't decided yet. I think I'll write a third verse about Pearl, then it can be about her."

"I was a writer too," she tells him. "In one of my lives. I wrote an ethical tract on the problem of good and evil as seen from different points of view. Unfortunately no one would publish a philosophy book by a woman in the eighteenth century.

"You know, Lux, you always did look a little strange but in this life you've excelled yourself. I see you were created for the day colourful hair dye was invented."

She goes off to help make a cup of tea with her friend, whose flat it is.

Lux looks in the mirror to see if the bandage matches his hair. He is quite pleased with it. Sort of piratical. He kicks his legs around, looking for something to do. Rummaging around in his carrier bag he finds the robot and the battery but when he sets it up it still doesn't work.

"Some major malfunction in the circuitry," he mutters, displeased, imagining himself briefly as an important local expert on robotics. A copy of the demo tape falls into his fingers and he chuckles. This demo tape will never see the light of day if he can help it. Ignorant, unartistic, thrashing motherfuckers.

He notices that his nail varnish is chipped.

"Another indignity," says Lux to Kalia, who brings him some tea. "I know for a fact that Chaucer had a personal manicurist to make sure his nails were in perfect condition before he sat down to write *The Canterbury Tales*."

"Stop rambling, Lux."

Lux stops rambling and finds the Mary Luxembourg manuscript in his carrier bag. He doesn't know how it got there. He must have absent-mindedly pocketed it some time when he was around Nicky. He pulls it out for a read.

"What a bunch of garbage," he decides, halfway through the first page, and hunts for his crayon to make some much-needed alterations.

"I killed my computer, I killed my computer," mumbles Nicky hopelessly, in the ambulance. "I killed my computer. It's haunting me. They're trying to artificially inseminate me. The country's full of rapists trying to get at me."

Pearl wakes.

"Where's my film?" she asks immediately.

Nicky shakes her head hopelessly. "It got lost somewhere along with the burning fire engine."

"Oh for fuck's sake," explodes Pearl. "Let me out of this ambulance."

"When I find Lux," rasps Grub to Eugene, "I am going to kill him. No messing about, I'm going to tear his fucking head off."

"Maybe if we tear it off soon we can get some of our coke back."

"Yeah. I'll teach him to fuck around with the Jane Austen Mercenaries."

The Jane Austen Mercenaries? thinks Johnny, who is hiding round the corner with a sophisticated listening device. Who are they?

"Fucking hell, this is grim," says Lux, appalled at Mary Luxembourg's novel. "Whoever wrote this wants to be rolled around in barbed wire."

He starts ripping pieces out of the manuscript, pencilling through lines and adding his own, writing poems in the margins and editorial comments all over the place that completely obscure the script. By the time I finish, this will be a masterpiece, he thinks, busily scribbling away.

Kalia glances out of the kitchen window. Down below she catches a glimpse of someone who looks very much like a descendant of Heaven hurrying by.

IN THE FIFTEENTH CENTURY Kalia has the misfortune to be born in the middle of a rash of terrible witch hunts.

As a servant of the Witchfinder she is expected to take notes on witches prior to them being burned at the stake.

Unable to do this, she tries to help them escape.

"You will never get back into Heaven this way," says the voice of god to her, in a dream. You are meant to be doing good, not breaking the law."

"I am doing good. I'm helping people escape when they are about to be horribly killed."

"But you are still breaking the law. And you are being disloyal to your employer who is, after all, doing good, in his opinion."

"Well every good deed could be interpreted two ways if you are going to look at it like that," protests the dreaming Kalia.

"True."

"So how am I meant to know what acts of kindness are actually kindnesses?"

"It's a difficult problem," says god.

We Get Your Man Personnel and Ace Headhunters are now both com-
peting madly for Sebastian Flak. With queries pouring in about him all
the time they know he must be something special. Neither of them has
ever heard of him before but there have been so many requests for his
services that they figure he must be an accounting genius.

"Get me Flak at any cost," demands the head of Ace Headhunters.
"He is becoming one of the most sought-after men in the business. I
pay you to keep up with affairs, not provide me with a lot of third-raters
while the big fish slip through the net. Now go out and make contact."

"Maybeline," says Sebastian, on the phone, "about this chanting. It's
starting to make me feel funny. I'm getting visions."

"Nonsense," says Maybeline endearingly. "I don't get any visions."

"Right," agrees Sebastian. "Neither do I."

The ambulance carrying Pearl and Nicky comes to a temporary halt,
unable to pass a burnt-out bus in the middle of the road.

Now's my chance, thinks Pearl. I'll make a run for it.

Beside her Nicky has gone quiet.

On the other hand, thinks Pearl, maybe I should stay here with
Nicky. She should be in hospital. If I go and try to find my film she is
bound to follow me. The humane thing would definitely be to stay here
with Nicky and go to the hospital.

The ambulance door opens and a policeman's head appears. To hell
with the humane thing, thinks Pearl, and sprints out the back.

"I'm feeling better," she calls over her shoulder. Nicky runs after her,
unable to face going to a hospital on her own.

There is rioting going on in this street and they have to duck their
way through some flying stones and then round a huge circular rubbish
skip that has been set alight and pushed into the road.

Kalia has finished bandaging Lux's head and talks to her friend
Marion.

"It must be bad for you living here with a riot going on, especially as the hospital placed you here to help you work your way back into normal community life."

Marion shrugs.

"Noise, violence, police cars roaming about, broken windows. Much the same as usual."

"What are you doing here, ghost among these urns, these film-wrapped sandwiches and help yourself biscuits," says Lux. "Or how did you get this flat?" He looks up briefly at the boarded windows.

"Special housing needs," says Marion. "The council gave it to me when I came out of the mental hospital. It is meant to be good for me, running my own home, although as I'm not much good at plumbing and the repairmen have taken seven months to fix the hot water I'm finding it a bit difficult. Still, you could say I'm back to normal life."

Sebastian, meeting with We Get Your Man Personnel all arranged, slips incognito onto a 159 bus which will take him from his home in St. John's Wood down to Brixton, a highly suitable area for a meeting because there he will be unrecognised. He understands that secrecy is essential.

"What are you doing?" asks Kalia, bringing Lux a sandwich.

"Revising my novel. Thank you for the sandwich."

She looks at him. "Well, someone else's novel," he admits. "But I am doing them a favour, it is a dreadful novel. The author has the soul of a pterodactyl."

Kalia laughs and cuts up some more sandwiches.

She has a slightly disquieting habit of appearing to do some internal calculation whenever she does anything for anyone, but apart from that Kalia exudes wisdom.

"Pearl would like it now. I've put in some poems about her."

121

"That reminds me of the perfume-guessing contest," she says.
"What?"

"Something you were involved in in a previous life. Do you think I am rambling stupidly?"

"Certainly not," replies Lux, politely accepting another sandwich and waiting a second while Kalia does some brief mental arithmetic. "If you say you met me in the past, I believe it. What happened?"

"I can't go on," moans Nicky, and sits down on the pavement.

"What d'you mean you can't go on?" demands Pearl. "We have to find my film."

"I hurt. I can't go on." With some difficulty Pearl checks back a flood of abuse. Given a choice between her lover dying in the middle of the riot and recovering her film she is not entirely sure which she would take.

"Have you seen Lux?" demands Eugene, appearing through some smoke.

"Go fuck yourself," snarls Pearl, having more important things to think about.

The veins and tendons stand out in her neck, as they do when she is angry.

"So," says Kalia to Lux, "after you helped win the first round of the perfume-guessing contest you were the hero of the moment. The family stuffed you full of so much rice, fish and sake you looked like you might burst. Of course you had been wandering around starving for years so this was understandable.

"But you, fairly stupidly, insisted on trying to win the hand of the eldest daughter of the household, Shimono, and she was already betrothed to the Emperor's nephew."

Lux, sitting beside Kalia as she speaks, is enthralled at hearing a story about himself.

"Also, there were problems brewing. The head of the opposing forces was Yasmin. He was lord of the next hamlet and sort of non-playing captain of their team. Not only was he determined to thwart any act of kindness I could commit, he was continually obsessed with making any life he had as successful as possible so he wasn't going to let you get away with beating his perfume squad. It was his intention to make his team the most famous in all Japan, thereby coming to the attention of the Emperor and gaining an appointment as chief perfume coach in Tokyo, a highly prestigious position.

"The next day he put poison in one of the perfume vials before it was passed to you—some Ethiopian musk, if I remember correctly. But fortunately I had predicted this very event and was able to divert the bowl away from you. And after this you went on to guess every single aroma correctly again and won the next round of the contest.

"Yasmin was furious, although formal etiquette prevented him from showing it. Worse, Shimono, always a woman of poor taste, began to be attracted to you because of the heartbreakingly romantic poems you kept getting me to stuff under her door every night . . ."

Sebastian, unused to travelling by bus, does not enjoy the journey very much but cheers himself up with thoughts of the telling-off he gave the Chief Accountant the previous day after being warned that his work was no longer up to scratch.

"Oh yes?" he had said. "Well, let me tell you, Mr. so-called Chief Accountant, that I am the one person in this company with any future, possibly excepting some of the sperm in the scientific department. Soon I won't need to bother about you or your damn company."

And with that he buried his head in *Soldier of Fortune* magazine, no longer bothering to hide it inside a *Financial Times*, so confident was he of being headhunted at any moment and whisked off into the major league of company directors, where it is quite possible to award yourself a pay rise that gives you in one year more money than is taken home in a lifetime by one of your employees.

Over at the scientific department gloom has set in. Despite Mr. Socrates pressing ahead with the arrangements for the beauty contest, trapped now in his own publicity, there is no way that the grand artificial insemination ceremony can go ahead without the genetic programme.

"Couldn't we fake it?" he suggests. Dr. Carlson is not enthusiastic. As a scientist he has strong ethical objections to faking things.

16

Lux, SLUMPED thoughtfully in a chair, sits upright, eyes widening so violently that he flakes off a few pieces of mascara.

"Pearl is somewhere close."

"She can't be. She has gone away to hospital."

"No," says Lux frantically. "I can smell her organic moisturising cream. She must have come back to look for me."

He stands, gathering his coat about him.

"I'm really enjoying your story. But I must get out and look for Pearl."

"You are obsessed with her."

"Yes."

"She doesn't seem all that keen on you."

"Yes she does. She resents me a little because I am so good looking and I improved her film and I wasn't sympathetic enough when she told me she was sad about all the witches being burned in the fifteenth century. She spends a lot of time thinking about that. Did you know they used to burn witches?"

"I'd heard about it."

"And of course she is busy chaperoning a manic depressive

companion around, but I think I'm winning her over. Good looks are bound to win out against sick friends."

"You keep insulting Nicky."

"She's sick."

"Maybe. But it was quite heroic of her, half destroying the company like that."

Lux shrugs, not impressed by heroism if it comes from his rival.

"Shouldn't you stay here in safety?"

"It's alright. I'll be fine. Riots are no problem unless you happen to be a victim and I was born too lucky to be a victim. Pearl needs me. Thanks for bandaging up my head. Does the bandage suit me?"

"Perfectly," smiles Kalia, who has long knowledge of Lux's incredible vanity and a fair idea of why Pearl may not be falling all over him. Still, she likes him. She always did and she is pleased to meet him again. Throughout all her lifetimes she has bumped into him often and he is always the same, never doing anything except wandering around on his own singing or writing poetry and trying to convince people of his huge talent, always in vain.

She laughs out loud, remembering the occasion when Lux panicked a field full of saffron-robed monks chanting sutras in the presence of the Buddha by trying out a few free-form variations of his own at maximum volume. Some people said afterwards that it was the only time since his enlightenment that the colour actually drained from the Buddha's cheeks, but this was probably an exaggeration.

"I'll come with you," she says, getting her coat. "You need someone to look after you. Also you are a prime candidate for receiving acts of kindness. Helping you out a few more times might get me back into Heaven. And I'm anxious to learn something about this heavenly descendant."

"The one the birds told you about?"

"That's right."

"I talk to birds too, sometimes. They seem like quite sensible creatures, just flying around enjoying themselves all the time. Do you think you'll meet this heavenly descendant?"

"I've already seen him. Out of the kitchen window."

They head for the door.

"Put back everything you've stolen," says Kalia.

"Right," says Lux, emptying his pockets of Marion's pearl earrings and a few other trinkets.

Outside he sniffs the air.

"This way," he says.

Pearl drags Nicky on.

"It's no use," says Nicky, who can't hunt anymore. Driven by desperation to lying, she tells Pearl that she saw her film consumed by a piece of burning fire engine.

Pearl, depressed, slumps against a wall.

They stay there for a while, both bleeding slightly from their cuts, ignoring the still active crowds walking up and down the broken pavements.

Mike appears. He has come out of Liberation Computers to see if the riot is still raging.

Seeing Pearl and Nicky standing forlornly by the wall, he offers them some shelter in the Enterprise Centre, which they accept.

"Look," says Lux, halting close to where the fire engine is still smouldering.

"A carrier bag. I like carrier bags, I used to collect them." He starts rummaging around in it, emptying it out so that rolls of paper start tangling round his legs. Always sensitive about any stray body harming his legs, he reaches down to free them.

"What's this?" Unravelling it reveals the paper to be some sort of computer programme. Underneath is a roll of film in a can.

"Look, Kalia, it's Pearl's film. It must've got left here when she got took off in the ambulance."

The film, along with Nicky's bag, has survived the heat from the burning fire engine, protected by a sheet of asbestos removed from the roof of the flats by a sub-contractor and illegally dumped in the skip.

"So," growls Patrick, watching on television as an incident-seeking camera swings round to show Mike helping Pearl and Nicky inside the Enterprise Centre. "He's picking up women in the street now. First Lux and now this. The man is disgusting. It wouldn't surprise me if he was a closet heterosexual."

Lux is overjoyed.

Now he can take the film to Pearl and she will practically fall all over him with gratitude because it is her most treasured possession.

The film is quite precious to Lux as well because he liked playing the part of the scarecrow and imagines that when people see it they will bombard him with offers to come and read them some poetry. Possibly he will be spotted by Hollywood.

"Few great poets have gone to Hollywood. I will be a sensation."

He is already sensational as the scarecrow, or so he tells everyone. He wrote a special scarecrow poem for it which Pearl wouldn't let him use, but he is still sensational.

Kalia crosses the street to help a man who is trying to fix his front door back on its hinges and Lux takes the opportunity to examine the rest of Nicky's bag. The genetic programme is all written in scientific data and means nothing to him. Then there is a diary, some tampons, a book, a few pens, and finally a memo on Happy Science notepaper. Finding nothing worth pocketing, Lux is a little disappointed. He reads the memo.

To: the Chairman
From: Dr. Carlson

Please ensure that Sebastian Flak does not come anywhere near my laboratory anymore. He may for all I know be a great accountant but he is interfering with our work.

Nicky had gathered up the memo by accident in her rush to leave Happy Science with the programme.

Kalia returns.

"Why are these musicians chasing you?" she asks.

"What musicians?"

"The ones I hid you under a bush from. The ones coming round that corner."

Sebastian walks round the corner from the centre of Brixton to the slightly upmarket restaurant in Acre Lane and waits for his rendezvous. To his surprise and consternation, a riot starts outside.

Mike and Marcus of Liberation Computers make Pearl and Nicky welcome, in between standing guard with a hosepipe inside their small office in the Enterprise Centre. They are determined that, come what may, Liberation Computers will not be burned to the ground.

While they are drinking tea Gerry and Mark appear. Gerry has come to see how Liberation Computers are coping with the riot. He knows about them from an article he did in *Uptown* on left-wing computer groups. Actually Liberation Computers was the only one in existence but he managed to make it sound better by exaggerating a bit.

"Nicky," he cries ecstatically, "I've been looking for you all over."

"I still won't go out with you," Nicky tells him, staring at the floor.

"The manuscript," says Gerry, ignoring this. "Mary Luxembourg's book. I left it at your house. Can I have it back?"

Nicky doesn't reply. She is plunging in and out of a walking nightmare about dead computers and living rapists.

"It's gone," Pearl tells him. "Burned up by a blazing fire engine down in Stockwell. And my film."

"Have you come to report on Liberation Computers again?" enquires Marcus in the friendly manner people put on when a reporter comes to say something nice about them.

"Later," replies Gerry. "Right now I have to find a phone."

The Jane Austen Mercenaries appearing in the middle distance, Lux and Kalia quickly disappear back into the estate. A huge rabbit warren, the estate is good to hide in, good to get attacked in, good to make TV programmes about, good to discuss from a distance, good to riot in, good to do everything in except live.

"What a disgusting place," says Kalia. "Whatever induced anyone to build it?"

"A modern red-brick metropolis of urine-soaked walkways and concrete play areas," says Lux, adapting freely from one of his poems. "I wish I had a drink," he continues, a little unsteadily now as his mind becomes slightly detached.

"Excuse me a second. I'm just going down there to help that person who is limping." Kalia disappears.

"What are you doing here?" demands a voice.

It is Johnny and his patrol, scouting the area.

"I am here on private business," replies Lux.

"You don't look like a businessman."

"I am an associate of Sebastian Flak, a well known and talented accountant," claims Lux, mind fixing onto the memo he has just read.

"I am putting him in touch with the Jane Austen Mercenaries, a local thrash metal band who I believe need some tax advice after reaching number one with their new record following some favourable reviews from Lux, the big music critic."

"Really," says Johnny.

Lux, seeing that he has gained an interested audience, makes up a little more. "Of course, the whole thing could be a cover story for something different. I believe the Jane Austen Mercenaries are being hunted by the police for some reason. Possibly they are criminals. I know for a fact that Eugene used to be a thief before moving into industrial espionage. This conflict of interests is the reason they produce such fascinating music, along with the fact that Lux the Poet writes all their lyrics. He was voted top lyricist last year by four music papers. Would you like to hear an example of his work?"

"Not right now," says Johnny, and leads his men off round the corner where he calls Mr. Socrates on his mobile phone.

"You were right," he tells him. "There is a Sebastian Flak connection. I've just met his associate. I'll tail him. Can you see if you can find me any information about the Jane Austen Mercenaries? That is the code name being used by the other people involved. It seems to be a sizeable organisation. It sounds to me like they must have the genetic programme."

"I just met someone interesting," says Lux as Kalia returns.

"So did I."

"Who?"

"Menelaus."

"Who's that?"

"The descendant of Heaven."

"What was he doing?"

"Limping. I helped him."

"Where is he now?"

"He limped off. He wouldn't let me help him anymore. I'll try and watch out for him as long as he is around."

Kalia is close by, Johnny, or Yasmin, realises. He can sense it. He laughs unpleasantly.

He also knows that Kalia thinks she is close to one million acts of kindness. He also knows that she has in fact passed one million some lifetimes ago. But she is not getting back into Heaven. Ever. His master, the evil prince, is forging the figures. She will never make her total, no matter how long she tries.

"What is it Nicky keeps mumbling?" asks Mike.

"Computer police," Pearl tells him. "According to her we are being pursued by some organisation called Personal Computer Services."

Mike and Marcus gather round eagerly.

"You're actually being pursued by the Personal Computer Services? The computer police? Don't worry, we'll help you. They are our arch-enemies. We've been waiting for an opportunity to fight them."

Mike starts programming something into a terminal.

"Incidentally," he calls over his shoulder. "Haven't I seen you round with Lux?"

"Only when I couldn't escape in time," says Pearl. "Why?"

"Oh, nothing. He just stole all my personal belongings and ruined my relationship with my boyfriend, that's all."

"I can well believe it. The only reason he doesn't have everything I owned is because my house burned down before he could carry it away. I caught him one time sneaking out in my best leather jacket with the pockets crammed full of everything I hadn't nailed down. He claimed he was only taking my aspirins because he had a headache but I knew he was going to mash them up with my soap and set his hair with it. There is nothing that Lux won't try setting his hair with."

"Too right," says Mike, glumly. "I now know that with KY jelly you can make a spike two feet long and it stays in position perfectly."

Mike was exaggerating. Lux's hair currently stands around eighteen inches in all directions.

"Kalia. Seeing as you can predict the future, can't you just lead me right to Pearl?"

"I'm afraid not, Lux. Something is interfering. I can't see clearly at all. It has never happened before. I wonder if it might be Yasmin's doing. I feel he is somewhere around. Unless it is a sign that I am close to returning to Heaven."

"Is Heaven nice?"

"It's better than Brixton. And Camberwell."

"I stopped believing in god when I got a spot. I figured no divine being could be so cruel as to give me acne." He looks slightly worried. "Don't ever mention to anyone I had a spot, will you? It was only one and it went quickly."

"I won't."

"Promise?"

"Promise."

Lux relaxes. He trusts Kalia.

"Tell me more about Menelaus."

"He was the husband of Helen of Troy and Agamemnon's brother. This life he has come back as an accountant."

"What's he like?"

"Horrible. You met him before."

"When?"

"At the siege of Troy."

"Was I a hero?"

"Not exactly. As a foot soldier you went into the battle naked with only a sword and a shield and some greaves. You quite liked that, being vain, but when the Trojans attacked, you tried running off the battle-field. You still got hacked up into little pieces."

"Oh."

"I think it was that which made you stop being normal."

"Sounds reasonable. Who wants to get chopped up on a battlefield? So after that I spent three thousand years wandering around being a poet?"

"Yes. As well as never doing any work and having hopeless love affairs."

"Sounds to me like a series of solid achievements."

Somewhere nearby a car alarm goes off. The alarm will wail for twenty minutes, but with sirens everywhere, it will not deter anyone from removing the in-car entertainment, and maybe the engine.

Lux wonders about something for a little while.

"Does everyone go through all their lives being the same?"

"No. You are an exception. Other people are always different. It depends on what sort of place they are born in, mainly. Right now there is an accountant wandering around the area whose main concern is to be a bigger accountant, and he used to be Menelaus, King of Sparta. Lux, why are you crawling on your hands and knees?"

"So the person that lives up there doesn't see me."

"Why not?"

"She got upset when she found out I was sleeping with everyone else she knew. Insanely possessive. I was lucky to escape with my life."

"What happened?"

"I got backed into a corner and had to escape out the window. Fortunately there was a creeper outside and I shinned down it in safety. But it was very lucky. As far as I know it's the only creeper in Brixton. What happened next in the perfume contest?"

Gerry gets through to the editor of *Uptown* where everyone is in the office preparing for the riot edition.

"Re-run my Mary Luxembourg retrospective," he tells him.

"We're busy doing a special riot edition. What's the idea of constantly phoning up with your changing literary obsessions?"

"It is highly relevant to tonight's events," claims Gerry. "It is books like Mary Luxembourg's that cause riots. Now be sure and print it or I'll tell everyone all about the way you treat your girlfriend."

JOHNNY IS FINDING the situation difficult. They are meant to be a secret organisation but in the riot you walk down one street and you get a brick over your head, then in the next you're being photographed by a hundred newsmen. They can't afford to have their pictures in the newspapers. They might end up as highly publicised as the SAS.

"I think it's time to take action, men. We can't hang around here all night. If some nigger attacks me with a petrol bomb I'll shoot him dead and that will be bad publicity for us. I think the key to the problem is this bunch calling themselves the Jane Austen Mercenaries. Have you noticed how they all have utterly filthy leather jackets but speak with Oxford accents? They are obviously frauds. And from the information I tricked out of that associate of Flak it seems likely that they have the programme and probably know the whereabouts of the computer killer. So let's get them."

He tries phoning in another report but finds that his line to Happy Science is no longer operative.

"What you doing?" asks Pearl.

"Interfering with the computer police line to headquarters," says

Mike, dialling some numbers and placing his computer phone in its modem. "Ought to cause them some problems."

He expects that this will cheer Pearl up. She bursts into tears.

"What's wrong?"

"Everything. Nicky in a coma. People being raped. And I've lost my film."

"Can't you make another?" enquires Mike kindly.

"No I cannot make another," screams Pearl. "Don't be so fucking stupid. I'm still a thousand pounds short of finishing this one. It has been awful. My backer has fucked me around, the cameraman didn't take me seriously and ended up spoiling some film and Lux pestered me for three months to let him into the act. I admit he wasn't bad in it but he kept spouting poetry when he was meant to be dead.

"In the final dramatic scene he was carried in as a corpse and, no warning given, valuable film running, he sat up and started quoting *Paradise Lost.* He was up to line sixty-seven before I could shut him up." The memory is too painful and her voice trails off.

"What did you do?"

"Clapped him round the head. He said he was just trying to show me he actually knew it."

The Jane Austen Mercenaries prowl the streets, as far as it is possible to prowl with a riot going on. Sometimes they are forced to run and sometimes they are held up by a roadblock.

On their travels they meet some members from another band who tell them that they are just out gathering material for lyrics for a song they plan to record first thing in the morning, unless the cheap-rate recording studio for the unemployed has been burned down.

Spurred on by this disastrous news they search even more frantically, but are interrupted suddenly by the arrival of Personal Computer Services.

"I'd like a word with you," says Johnny.

"No time," they say, and try to pass.

"I know you have the programme. You think I'm bluffing? I received the news from Flak's confederate. The one with red and yellow hair and a disgustingly effeminate face."

"Lux?"

"C'mon," says Grub. "We don't have time for this."

"Search these men," orders Johnny.

A fight ensues.

The Jane Austen Mercenaries put up good resistance but they are no match for the computer police, who are all trained for this sort of thing.

Sebastian wants to hide in the restaurant but it closes and all the customers have to leave and then the tube station shuts and the roads get blocked so he can't get on a bus and with the riot growing in ferocity he starts to panic.

"Yasmin set out to bribe the judges," continues Kalia to Lux as they walk through the estate. "He paid them to say that your guesses were incorrect when really they were right. I was powerless to help although I knew what was going on. As a result they pulled even in the contest.

"The Yamamoto family were distraught. They suspected cheating as well, but nothing could be proved. You were also distraught because you thought, fairly stupidly, that Shimono wouldn't like you so much if you didn't win the contest. You needn't have worried. Though she had poor taste in lovers, she was much too sensible a woman to bother about who won a perfume-guessing contest—"

"Now we've got you!" screams Eugene, appearing from an ambush round the corner. "Prepare to die."

Having been beaten up and searched by Johnny's men, the band are in an even more foul temper.

There is nowhere for Lux to run. He is surrounded.

"Well, hello," he says, blithely. "I've been looking all over for you. Where have you been?"

"Give us back our demo tapes."

"That is just what I wanted to see you about. While I was in your flat, saving you all from being arrested for possessing cocaine, at some risk to myself, there was a phone call from a record producer. He was frantic to put out your record and wanted the demo tape right away. I was just about to bring it to him when some desperate PR men from a rival company burst in through the door, demanding the tape. They claimed they had first rights on it. Of course I put them off because I could see they were criminals and then when I went out to take your tape to the real record executive I scrawled a fake message on the wall in case the criminals came back."

He beams at them.

"Unfortunately the riot prevented me making the rendezvous. I kept looking for you to give me some help but you were nowhere around. You're going to have to be a lot more dedicated if you want to make it in the music industry, you know. It's no good running around enjoying yourselves all the time when people are working hard to help your careers."

"I don't believe a word of it," protests Grub. "Where are the tapes now?"

"I was coming to that. The bad PR men caught up with me just outside Kalia's flat. Isn't that true?"

Kalia nods.

"They stole all the tapes. They claim you have a contract with them."

"We don't have a contract with anyone."

"Some record companies will stop at nothing."

"What were they like?"

Lux describes Johnny and his men.

"We did meet some people like that," says the drummer.

"I'm going to search you anyway," says Eugene. "And if I find the tape in that bag I'm going to rip your throat out."

Very fortunately, at that moment, a transit van full of police pulls up.

"What's going on here?" demands the driver, leaning out of the door.

"Nothing," replies Lux, pulling out the genetic programme from his bag. "I am just checking the riot damage on this estate against these plans here. I am a surveyor from Lambeth Council."

The police look at him doubtfully. He doesn't look like a surveyor. Still, Lambeth council is notorious for employing all sorts of strange people and he might have sneaked in under their equal opportunities policy.

Two policemen leave the van and order them up against a wall where they are searched in case they are looters. Finished with before the musicians, Lux slips the tapes to Kalia.

An urgent message on the radio draws the police away.

"So you see," says Lux, opening his carrier bag wide, "I no longer have the tapes. They were stolen, despite my heroic attempts to save them."

"What's going on?" says the leader of a police foot patrol, appearing in the wake of the van. The area is now crawling with policemen.

"Nothing," says Lux, sidling round the corner with Kalia.

They flee.

"Lux, you are the most terrible liar."

"Yes," agrees Lux. "It's because I'm a poet. All poets are liars."

"I'd agree with that. I have met a lot through the ages."

"It must've been interesting, living for thousands of years. Have you met any famous people?"

"A few. Mostly I was a peasant. I did meet Genghis Khan and Plato and Catherine the Great and some Incas and Aborigines you wouldn't have heard of, Confucius and St. Augustine, both prigs, Wild Bill Hickock, Mary Queen of Scots, Betty Grable . . ."

"What?" explodes Lux, finding this hard to believe. "You're actually telling me you met Betty Grable?"

"Certainly. I was a make-up artist for Twentieth Century-Fox."

Lux comes to a halt, gaping.

"Stop standing there with your mouth open," says his companion. "We should be moving along."

Nicky comes briefly out of her coma.

"Pearl, I never mentioned it before but the stills I took for you from Happy Science for your film were pictures of illegal genetic experiments on cells and foetuses. They'll probably kill you to get them back."

She sinks back into a trance.

"Wonderful," grunts Pearl. "This is just what I need."

"Where is the film now?" asks Mike, taking a break from trying to penetrate the computer police mainframe and wipe their memory banks.

"Burned."

"Never mind. We will at least put Personal Computer Services off the trail."

In this Mike is being a little optimistic. Liberation Computers are more used to doing things like running up mailing lists for Nicaraguan support groups and telling people how to break into banking systems than actually trying to fight anyone, and while they are doing their best by way of fouling up the computer police's links to HQ and sending out signals to wipe their memory banks, Mike has a definite notion that this is as far as the conflict will go—each side vying with the other in computer expertise.

The computer police, however, are only interested in technical expertise to a certain extent. They are more interested in hitting people and if they catch up with Liberation Computers and find them sheltering Nicky and Pearl then they will be quite prepared to tear them into bite-sized pieces.

Sebastian can't believe he has got caught up in a riot and he can't understand why the police are unable to quell it immediately and he doesn't know where to go for safety.

Mercifully, in order to remain incognito, he has worn some old clothes instead of an expensive suit. He imagines that anyone coming to Brixton in an expensive suit would be torn to pieces.

He tries leaving the area but every time he turns a corner he seems to find himself facing a platoon of policemen and he is soon lost and confused.

18

IN THE HAPPY SCIENCE LABORATORIES gloom still reigns.

"We hear rumours of some problems," says a journalist on the phone to Dr. Carlson. "Is it true that you tried to force one of your employees to be artificially inseminated and she went crazy and smashed the place up? And isn't this cheating? Wasn't there meant to be a contest to find a mother?"

"It is all lies," barks the Doctor and raps the phone down. On his knee is a roughed-out genetic chart but he knows in his heart that it is useless. He can never make another one in time.

Anyway, you can't really rough out a genetic chart. Certainly not to Nobel Prize–winning standards.

The riot grumbles on, although in most places the police are starting to get the upper hand as reinforcements from all over London and the surrounding counties succeed in completely isolating Brixton from the rest of the world and dragging more people away into vans where they are shuttled off to holding cells in police stations all over the capital.

But they later protest that what they really need to deal with the riot effectively is a law that allows them to drag absolutely everyone away and would the government mind passing one as soon as possible, and this is only sensible, of course, because if the whole population of Brixton is dragged away to prison then there certainly won't be any more riots.

The Enterprise Centre is a refurbished department store full of small shops in the front and small offices upstairs, including Liberation Computers, where Gerry now returns after making his call to *Uptown*.

Mike engages him in conversation. He has found it difficult getting much conversation out of Pearl or any at all out of Nicky.

"What've you been doing since I last saw you?"

"Oh, working, doing reviews, that sort of thing. I'm assistant editor of *Uptown* now. It's no easy life, you know, you wouldn't believe the amount of garbage I have to come into contact with. Last week I reviewed twenty-five novels."

"Incredible," says Mike. "How do you manage it?"

"I only read every third page."

"Doesn't that make it difficult?"

"Not really. Sometimes I don't read them at all. You can generally get a pretty good idea of what they're about from the cover and maybe someone in the office knows something about them . . . Pretty good riot, eh?"

"I suppose so," says Mike, worried about his computers. "But I'm scared someone might smash up this place and ruin all our work."

"Most unlikely," Gerry reassures him. "After all, you are not oppressors. No one engaged in a riot against government brutality is going to harm a left-wing gay-orientated computer firm, are they?"

"So," says Grub, sweating from the exertions of the night. "Who does have the demo tape?"

No one is sure. Time is running out. If they can't deliver it to the

record executive the next day he will find another Brixton band and
have them put out the fashionable single.

"It's all your fault."

"What d'you mean it's my fault?" protests Eugene.

"You left him alone in the house."

"Well how come I was responsible for all the demo tapes?"

"You wanted to be. No doubt so you could show off your singing. Not that anyone cares much about the singing in a thrash metal
band."

"Shut up," says Eugene, wearily. "God, I'm fed up with this fucking
riot."

"We've got some good publicity shots."

"True."

"Look." Eugene points past the wreckage of a customised fifties
Ford that was once somebody's pride and joy. "There are the people that
attacked us. Did you notice how Lux knew exactly what they looked
like?"

"They look horrible."

"They could well be from a record company."

"I'm going to have a word with them," says Eugene bravely.

A police car screeches past Lux and Kalia, siren wailing, driver looking
grim-faced and important.

"'What mad pursuit? What struggle to escape?

What pipes and timbrels? What wild ecstasy?'

"That's Keats," he tells his companion. "A good poem, though I
have no idea what a timbrel is. Possibly it was something he just made
up for effect. Did you really know Betty Grable?"

"Yes."

Having been a make-up artist for Twentieth Century Fox, Kalia is
now Lux's hero.

"Was she nice?"

"Yes. Very. But generally the nicest people were the peasants. I didn't really like many of the famous ones."

They walk on in silence for a while, but Lux has an urge to talk.

"Brixton is in chaos," he says out loud to the whole world. "All around buildings burn whilst police and rioters battle it out. Somewhere in the darkness a hell-spawned band of heavy metal thrashers are trying to inflict their dire music on an innocent public. Only Lux can stop them. Elsewhere unknown forces claiming to be computer police pursue their own nefarious ends and men in vans try to stuff diamond rings down the throats of harmless onlookers."

His voice gets louder. "Meanwhile Pearl is sinking in a swamp of utter helplessness, partly of her own making, obstinately refusing the help of Lux, the only person standing in the way of total disaster, striding gamely through every trouble that life throws at him and laughing in the face of adversity. Lux, hero of film and poetry notebook, shining spirit, guardian of artistic sensibilities, fearless pursuer after . . ."

"Shut up Lux," says Kalia, and stoops to help a young child back onto her bicycle.

"I can't help it. I'm bored."

"We're in the middle of a riot."

"I'm bored with the riot."

"People are suffering."

"I'm bored with people suffering. Anyway none of them like my poetry. They deserve to suffer. Look, a kebab shop. It's burning. Good."

They observe the smouldering remains for a while.

"Always seemed like a strange idea to me," says Lux. "Cutting up a harmless sheep then cramming it into a bit of bread with a few tomatoes and onions. I hate the thought of all these sheep getting made into kebabs. Completely barbaric. Where is Pearl? I'm desperate to find her."

He stumbles. Kalia looks at him, concerned. Blood is seeping out of his head wound.

"Did you meet Lana Turner?"

"Yes."

"I look like her. Tell me more of the perfume story."

Sebastian shakes his head to clear it of the smoke and flames and hallucinations. He is chanting to make things better but it is sending him into dreadful visions of past lives and this is no help at all while trying to dodge flying bricks.

"I'm going to scout the area," says Mike. "See if any of the computer investigators are about."

He leaves the Enterprise Centre. The main street is a total shambles. Piles and piles of broken glass lie among burning rags and smouldering tyres and shattered shop-fronts and everywhere there are bricks, stones or shards of pavement that have been used as missiles. Every shop has had its metal shuttering wrenched off, and inside, on the stripped counters, there remain only a few mangy items too unpleasant for anyone to even steal, like novelty watches or packets of instant noodles.

Down a sidestreet some firemen have to stand back as the front of a hi-fi shop crashes to the ground in flames, sending sparks and fragments of hi-fi equipment bouncing around on the pavement, a pavement recently re-tiled by the council in a futile attempt to improve the area. Unable to provide any jobs for the inhabitants, the nice new pink pavement is a gesture that receives little thanks.

Groups of people still walk around, as they do all night. The police are eventually able to control the riot but unable to completely clear the streets, even with their huge numbers, because the riot involves not just a few but a large part of the community, all the poor and dissatisfied who have long since given up hope of attracting any sort of attention to their plight and see the riot as an opportunity to do something positive.

Everyone is pleased at fighting back. Mike catches the violent community spirit and, walking along, he plans a special riot edition of the Liberation Computers Monthly Newsletter.

Round the corner in Acre Lane he is singled out from a group of people and robbed at knifepoint. He is only able to pull two pound coins out of his pocket and the muggers look fairly disgusted but take the two pounds anyway and after this Mike goes back to the Enterprise Centre a little confused and bitter because it seems to him that he was singled out because he was white and as a white socialist this is very hard to cope with.

What's more, when he gets back to Liberation Computers he is too embarrassed to mention it to his partner Marcus because Marcus is black and Mike thinks that Marcus might think he is getting at him in some way so he ends up by being extra friendly and acting like a fool.

A little reasoned discussion between Eugene and Johnny leaves everyone still suspicious of each other but fairly sure that Lux has been lying.

The Jane Austen Mercenaries resume their search, now quite seriously intending to murder him. Personal Computer Services slink back into the darkness to consider their next move.

"So," says Johnny to his men. "Everything points to this Lux person. He must know where the genetic programme is. Putting us onto these musicians was just a ploy. Let's get him."

Johnny is enjoying the riot. He always likes scenes of violence. As Yasmin, in every life he has four aims: to frustrate Kalia's good intentions, to frustrate everyone else's good intentions, to make himself as important as possible, and to participate in scenes of violence. He has no real desire to return to Heaven.

"The day before the final round of the perfume-guessing contest Shimono sent you a poem. You thought it was a terrible poem but, shamelessly hypocritical to the last, you told her it was a work of genius when you met her next day in the ceremonial garden."

"Sounds like the only thing to do," Lux interjects. "If you're in love with someone and they suddenly send you a poem you can hardly tell them it is rubbish, can you?"

"No, not unless you are honest. Anyway, at noon you all assembled for the final. By this time your nose was so finely trained you could spot a perfume in the next county. I have no idea why in all your lifetimes the only supreme ability you ever had was the ability to identify perfumes, but there you are. The ways of the gods are strange."

"It doesn't sound so bad. Better than going to war and cutting people up with a meat cleaver."

"True. Anyway, I tried to attend the final but Yasmin bribed a maid to smash some valuable dishes and then had me blamed for it. I was banished to my room. It was a terrible time. Just the day before I had been trying to help an old man across a stream and Yasmin leapt out and frightened us and the old man was drowned. So instead of an act of kindness to my credit I had a murder on my slate."

"Surely not. It wasn't your fault the man was killed. You still meant well."

"Not according to Yasmin. He claimed the old man was a fugitive from justice and I was helping him escape. No doubt the gods supported him in this. He was always more influential than me. Now stop interrupting. I was telling you about the final day of the perfume contest—"

"Lux!" comes a scream that is loud even by the standards of the night. "Give us the demo tape. I'm going to wrap my bicycle chain round your neck."

Lux, as keen on his neck as he is on the rest of him, looks for a wall to shin over.

No wall coming into view, he is forced to climb a tree, a sturdy nondescript type of tree planted in between housing blocks in the estate. Lux is not sure if he likes trees. He has a feeling that poets probably should but really he prefers concrete. Still, it serves a useful purpose now. Persistently vandalised, it has no branches near ground level and a smooth trunk that only someone as nimble as Lux could scale. While the Jane Austen Mercenaries gather round at the foot of the tree, unable to pursue him, Lux hardly notices the ascent.

Down below, not wanting to get into a fight with the band, Kalia slips unnoticed into a play area.

Lux finds a comfortable branch and glares down at his pursuers. A squirrel, cut off from its home in the park, frightened by the riot, hops over and joins him.

Amazing, thinks Lux. I am practically god-like. Even squirrels come to play with me, and squirrels are notably shy animals. Virtually a modern-day St. Francis of Assisi.

Lux is noted for the way animals tend to flock around him, though no one generally goes as far as comparing him to St. Francis of Assisi.

"It is a being of warmth, I think," he says to the squirrel. "That's a line from Stevie Smith. Do you like Stevie Smith? Yes? Good."

He hunts through his memory for a nice squirrel poem. Unable to find one he quotes a few lines of Kathy Acker:

"for you my love and me a few brief hours of sun
then no consciousness blackness perpetually.
take it kiss me do it grab me
grab my arm grab my ankles grab my cunt hairs—"

He looks up to check if the squirrel is paying attention. It is rapt.

Good, thinks Lux, obviously an animal of taste, and gets ready to quote the rest.

"Lux!"

The shout from below interrupts him. He looks down quizzically, having forgotten that the Jane Austen Mercenaries are at present clustered around the bottom of the tree, waiting for his blood.

"Give us back the tape. If you give us it back now we'll let you live."

"No chance," screams Lux. "You will only inflict it on people too weak to resist."

"Well what the fuck does it have to do with you what we do with it?"

"Someone has to protect the innocent. Your music is an abomination. I hate it. Worse, Pearl hates it. She thinks you are pigfuckers and no one that Pearl thinks is a pigfucker is going to get a demo tape back from me. Now leave me alone, I'm busy with a squirrel."

"He is stoned," mutters Eugene. "With all that coke inside him he's lost his mind. We'll just have to go and get it."

They start standing on each other's shoulders, trying to lay a hand on the nearest branch.

"One move closer and I'll feed your tape to the squirrel," bawls Lux, brandishing a copy. "And he's looking pretty hungry."

It is an impasse. The band settle down to starve him out. Round the corner the computer police watch, unsure of what is going on. Lux gets back to discussing poetry with his friend. Everyone is away rioting somewhere else and it is peaceful here, in the tree, apart from the distant drone of helicopters and the occasional thud of a sound system far over on the next block where an MC relentlessly ignores everything that is going on around him and practises his rapping through the night, too involved in it to even notice the riot, or the neighbours going crazy upstairs.

A POLICE TRANSIT VAN draws up beside a pub, the landlord unbolts his door and brings out a crate of beer bottles, and the police sergeant thanks him, loads up the beer bottles, and drives off.

Outside, Sebastian watches. Some youths brush past him. Did they jostle me deliberately, he wonders, scared.

There is an alleyway beside the pub so he creeps down it to think in peace but it goes wrong when what he thinks about is chanting his mantra to see if that will make things better and his fear and confusion make him plunge immediately into a terrible reincarnation memory where his job is to count the money left over from heretics after they have been burned and distribute the profits evenly between the inquisitors and himself. The character with yellow hair is about to be burned for spouting heretical poetry.

"I didn't know it was heretical," protests the figure, inglorious in death. "It was an accident, I won't do it again."

The same woman who figured as a nun in a previous vision comes to him and says she is going to help the poet to escape but needs a hundred gold doubloons to bribe the guards, but Sebastian won't lend it to her so the poet is burned and afterwards Sebastian is mortified because he realises that the reason he would not help to save him was because

153

he was attracted to him and if he was found out being attracted to a heretical male poet then burning would be the least he could expect.

He desperately shakes all this out of his head and tries to think what to do.

"It is hard being unappreciated," says Lux, to the squirrel. "And I am very unappreciated. No one likes my poems and Pearl won't fall in love with me. Never mind, soon I will be world champion poet and then they'll all be sorry."

He goes off into a daydream about a new carrier-bag collection. The squirrel goes to sleep.

Down below, Grub, now driven almost completely crazy with rage and frustration, refuses to wait any longer.

"I'm going to burn him out," he declares forcefully, and hunts around for something suitable to start a blaze.

On the far side of the small play area wall is an unignited petrol bomb.

"Is this wise?" says Eugene.

"I can't wait any longer. We need the demo tape. It could change our whole lives. I'm not letting stardom escape just because Lux decides to keep it. I'll have him out of there before he has time to destroy all the tapes."

Grub smashes the milk bottle round the base of the tree and the petrol soaks into the bark. He lights it.

Hm, thinks Lux, tree burning under him. An awkward situation, but no doubt I will be rescued soon.

Sure enough some police and firemen appear, fresh from combatting a terrible blaze in the next street. The firemen run over with a net and shout for him to jump. More importantly, a man with a TV camera on his shoulder is in close attendance.

Lux is pleased. He is bound to be on television now.

"Don't worry," he says to the squirrel, knowing that animals are scared of fire, "I'll save us."

He jumps down into the net, coat flowing up over his head and squirrel on his shoulder.

"Are you alright?" say the firemen, picking him out of the net.

"Fine, thank you," replies Lux, polite even in a crisis, and hurries over to the TV camera.

"Did you get some good pictures? I tried turning my best profile to the camera though it was a bit difficult with the tree burning and everything."

"Yes, we got some good pictures," says the cameraman. "Although you needn't have worried about your best profile because the squirrel's tail was covering up your face."

"What?"

Lux is outraged. He aims a kick at the animal but it is now out of range, heading for safety in the park.

"Two-timing little monster," he mutters, and stomps off, hands sunk deep into his pockets in disapproval.

The Jane Austen Mercenaries, meanwhile, have all been arrested for setting fire to a tree and are driven off in a Transit van.

Passing the flat where the sound system is still pumping it out, Lux directs a fierce scowl at the windows. Reggae sound systems are well down on the artistic approval list as far as he is concerned.

Johnny watches the arrest of the band with approval. It was him who brought the police here so quickly, calling them on his radio. He loves to see things going badly for people.

"Do you have anything to drink?"

Pearl feels like she needs something to cheer her up and calm her down. She has a sinking feeling in her stomach because she has lost the film, and with it eighteen months' work, in addition to all her possessions, which went up uninsured in her house. And also there is the matter of Happy Science apparently hot on her trail by way of Personal Computer Services, although she is still not entirely sure if she believes all this as Nicky is no longer a person you can really rely on, being either maniacally depressed or comatose.

"Yes," replies Mike. "We have a Liberation Computers emergency bottle of brandy. I'll get you some."

He offers some to Pearl in a cup.

"You want some, Marcus?"

"No thanks."

Marcus is busy working a computer.

"Go on, have some."

"No thanks."

"It's good brandy."

"I don't want it."

"Please have some brandy."

"What's the matter with you?" demands Marcus, exasperated, forced to turn round from his console where he was filling in time making up a new computer game.

"Nothing, nothing at all," cries Mike. "Why, was I acting like there was something the matter with me? I'm not acting any different than normal towards you, am I?"

Marcus wrinkles his face and turns back to his work. The game he is making is called "Together We Can Fight Imperialism!" and is a role-playing adventure centred on outwitting the CIA in Central America.

So far Liberation Computers adventure games have not been selling too well but home computer fans are notoriously indifferent to Trotskyism. "Re-live the Fourth International" lost them a terrible amount of money but they are still hopeful of breaking through.

Pearl abandons the cup for the bottle and starts pouring brandy down her throat.

Kalia observes Lux's rescue and is about to follow him when she is suddenly attacked by a dreadful wave of nausea. Forced to retreat into a shop doorway, she slumps to the ground. Her head is pounding.

What is causing it? She has never felt anything like it before. It feels as if someone is inside her skull, kicking.

Johnny phones in a report to Happy Science, although to do this he has to show some credentials to the police and use one of their telephones because his direct link has been cut off by Liberation Computers. They have lost Nicky and Pearl but are continuing to follow Lux, having meanwhile skirmished briefly with rioters and the Jane Austen Mercenaries.

"Any further progress?" asks Dr. Carlson, eagerly.

"Not really," Johnny tells him.

"Get me my genetic programme," snaps the Doctor, nerves starting to go, Nobel Prize for Science starting to fade from view.

"All right, don't shout," retorts Johnny, who is developing a headache.

There is a knock on the door. A cleaner comes in.

"Is this Mr. Sebastian Flak's office?"

"No it is not."

She leaves.

Odd, thinks Dr. Carlson. This is the third cleaner this evening who has been looking for Flak's office.

I need something to take my mind off things, he thinks, and gets on with some foetus experiments to calm himself down.

A young girl leans over a balcony. Maybe four years old when the Sex Pistols first rehearsed, she is wearing full punk regalia.

Lux wanders by.

"Hey," she calls, seeing him pass. "Whatya doing? Come on up."

Kalia's head clears slowly. Ignored by the people walking by, her thoughts begin to take shape. She can only assume that it is Yasmin's doing. He must have developed some way to attack her psychically, as well as blocking out her ability to see into the future. She knows that he is nearby.

She thinks about Heaven. I must be close to my total now. Very close. I hope so, I can't stand much more of it, and my incarnations are getting worse.

She could just about take the endless peasant lifetimes but the bed-sit in Camberwell has really got to her. She fights off another wave of nausea and presses on.

It is Sebastian who is responsible for Kalia's sickness. His subsonscious mind altered by continual chanting and his conscious mind now full of fear, he is unwittingly sending out dreadful waves of psychic disturbance.

Finely attuned to psychic disturbances, both Kalia and Yasmin are now suffering badly.

The young punk is attracted by Lux's spectacular looks, something Lux knows by instinct.

She makes him some tea.

"Have you seen Pearl?"

"Pearl who?"

Lux shrugs. "You wanna help me look for her?"

"No. What happened to your head?"

Lux can't remember.

The living room contains a modern sofa, an ashtray and nothing else. The sofa, a remnant of some previous tenants' abortive attempt to make the place comfortable, is now an unlovely affair of dented tubular metal and coffee-stained canvas.

The ashtray is a paint tin, another leftover from home improvements that came to a halt when the decorating grant from the social security was diverted into more enjoyable pursuits.

"We have done all we can," said Lord Yamamoto. "I have managed to change the judges for the contest. There will no longer be any biased decisions. It is now up to you, Chang Kwai Lux. The honour of the village rests in your hands."

The contestants file in amid formal ceremony, bowing to each other, accepting small bowls of tea laid out on the beautifully carved table that is the centrepiece of the room, the splendid showpiece room where Lord Yamamoto entertains his guests.

Lux discovers that the girl's name is Jean, she comes from Scotland, she is lonely in London, and she doesn't want to hear any of his poems, despite finding him irresistibly attractive. She wipes some damp blood from his cheek, kisses him, and they start fucking on the couch, adding a few more stains.

The perfumes are sent for. Everyone knows that today will be the most difficult of all, with scents gathered from all lands known to man.

"Greetings, Chang Kwai Lux," says Yasmin. "May you have the best of fortune in today's contest."

Lux makes his formally polite reply. He is not worried about the contest. He has the best sense of smell in the country.

"I would like to bring one thing to your attention," continues Yasmin, speaking softly so only Lux can hear. "I have in my possession three poems you have sent to Shimono, eldest daughter of the household. They are of a very intimate nature, as was her reply. Unless you lose the contest I will show them to Lord Yamamoto. His daughter being engaged to the Emperor's nephew, you will be lucky to escape with your head. If Shimono speaks up for you she will be banished to a monastery in the mountains. Here are the perfumes. Good luck in the contest."

Lux lies on the couch, body drained but mind still active with cocaine, pleased that Jean likes him.

She makes him some tea. Pearl always demands that he makes the tea.

"Not that I mind making tea of course," he mumbles. "I agree that tea making should be shared. I will do anything for Pearl."

"Are you in love with this person?" asks Jean, dressing.

"Yes."

"Would she mind you fucking someone else?"

"No. She wouldn't care. Anyway she is probably fucking her girlfriend at this very moment."

"Can two girls fuck?"

"I'm not sure. I may have chosen the wrong verb. But anyway, you know what I mean."

The riot has not reached up to this second-floor flat, and Jean has been unaffected by it, other than the sounds and smells that have made their way into her home, and Lux.

He is disappointed that she doesn't want to hear any of his poems.

Sebastian wanders blindly, dreadful visions pouring in and out of his head, weakly wishing that Maybeline was here to protect him in between running from attackers and pursuers, generally imagined. Despite his constant fear, he never actually meets anyone in the riot who wants to do him any harm, and his only injury is a twisted ankle that he inflicts on himself while running around in a panic.

But when he finds himself close to an exploding fire engine and a violent mêlée he runs off again in terror and haunts the walkways of an estate, hunting desperately for sanctuary.

Gerry leaves Liberation Computers to gather some more information for his riot article, making his way down towards Kennington where fighting is still going on. He sees a young woman being punched in the stomach as she is arrested and some people with scarfs round their faces making a last stand with stones and petrol bombs before being dispersed. The helicopter flies overhead, as it has done all night.

A police van tears past but is forced to halt in the distance where the road is partially blocked by an overturned car, and more police try to shepherd it through, although this is difficult as the group of rioters is still throwing missiles, some of which batter off the sides of the van.

Inside the van the Jane Austen Mercenaries sit in furious silence, each of them hating all the others, particularly Grub, whose idea it was to burn down the tree.

There is a brief thump on the door.

Jean looks through the spyhole to see what it is. Opening the door, she finds Sebastian slumped on the concrete.

He looks up, about to ask for shelter but, seeing the naked Lux in the background, a figure out of his nightmares, he moans dreadfully and passes out.

"That's funny," says Jean. "He looked at you and fainted."

"I often have this effect on people. Do you think we should help him?"

In the centuries following Kalia's life with the Witchmaster, she becomes less and less sure about what she is doing. Half the times she does some act of kindness it seems to her that maybe from someone else's point of view it is no kindness at all and sometimes in her dreams she has more converstions with Heaven and really they are no help whatsoever.

But, having no alternative, she carries on as best she can so that when she is born a Maori in New Zealand she tries helping all the sick Maoris who are dying of white men's diseases and then when she is a Tibetan priest she stays up all night saying extra prayers for the souls of the dead and during the Industrial Revolution in Britain she travels the country giving bread to all the people who have been dispossessed of their land and are starving in the new cities.

"It's all very well you giving them bread," a factory owner tells her, "but you are not helping anyone. If you give them free bread then they won't have to work. They'll sit around drinking all the time and the country will not become great."

Not convinced by this argument, Kalia keeps on handing out bread till she is thrown in prison as a subversive and transported to Australia, where she tries helping all the Aborigines who are dying of white men's diseases.

Jean is not all that keen on having a stranger in her flat and neither is Lux, who despite having met Sebastian at Happy Science does not recognise him. But after a while they decide that probably it will be all right if they give him a cup of tea, providing he wakes up.

Lux dresses.

"More tea?" asks Jean.

"Yes please."

"I'd make you a sandwich but next door borrowed my only knife for cutting up some smack and they haven't brought it back yet. I could get you some heroin if you want?"

"No thank you," says Lux. "I hate putting brown things up my nose."

Sebastian wakes from a dreadful nightmare, looks fearfully at Lux but more fearfully at the outside world, refuses a cup of tea, and asks Jean, without much hope, if she has a phone.

She dredges a phone out from under the sofa.

"This is private," he says.

"Well go somewhere else then," says Jean.

Sebastian glowers at them but makes his call. Lux's eyes glaze again and he starts mumbling some poems.

Kalia walks up through Brixton. The police let her through, deeming her harmless. The riot is quietening down, but her nausea is washing back and forward.

She halts. Johnny is in front of her, holding his head.

"Hello Yasmin," says Kalia.

"Is this your doing?" demands Johnny, eyes wild with sickness. They are both suffering at the hands, or mind, of Sebastian.

Well, muses Chang Kwai Lux, perfume being passed towards him in unmarked porcelain bowls. What is to be done? If I win the contest Yasmin will expose my relationship with Shimono.

But when he thinks about it the situation does not seem too bad. So what if everybody knows? Once Lux has won the perfume-guessing competition he will be the hero of the hour. Lord Yamamoto will be pleased to marry Shimono to him after he brings triumph to the hamlet. He can settle down to write poetry and eat rice in comfort. Possibly he can still do a little travelling.

For a poetic spirit there is only one thing to do and that is press on with the love affair. So he shoots a haughty glance at Yasmin, sitting regally behind his players, and starts reeling off the correct names of the perfumes.

"This one," he says, nonchalantly, "is Kubri, a distillation of flowers from the uncharted lands north of Tibet."

The crowd applauds. Lux bows gracefully.

While Sebastian is on the phone Lux suffers an unpleasant hallucination of going naked into battle. Fatigued, he sits on the floor.

"I have to hunt for Pearl. But I'm tired."

"I got some blues," says Jean. "Do you mind blue drugs?"

"No. Blue drugs are fine."

Lux swallows the tablets.

"I couldn't make the rendezvous," Sebastian explains on the phone. "I got caught up in the riot."

"You are close to Heaven, Kalia."

"I know."

"But I'll keep you on Earth for a while."

"You will not."

"I will. I have already delayed your return by hundreds of years.

Fool. Wandering around doing acts of kindness." Yasmin laughs.

But the confrontation is hampered by the pain and sickness that both of them are feeling, and Johnny's men, not knowing what is happening, help their leader away, leaving Kalia standing confused in the street.

"I was just arranging a business meeting," says Sebastian, feeling some need to explain. "I am being hunted by some big American companies for my accounting skills."

"I've met you before," says Lux, mind invigorated by the blues. "I remember, outside Happy Science. You weren't no help to me getting in the genius project. How about if I read you some of my poems now? I'm an even better poet than I was two months ago, I got lots of great new material, all night I've been giving interviews for television. They're practically fighting each other to give me my own programme. Any chance of putting in a good word for me?"

"I'll do my best," lies Sebastian, still horrified to meet the figure who has appeared in his nightmare visions. Only his massive desire to be recruited by Coca Cola is keeping him going.

"Where is the Enterprise Centre? I have arranged to meet my contact there."

"I'll show you. I have to get out and look for Pearl. You wanna help me?"

"I'm too busy."

"How about you?" He turns to Jean. She shakes her head, not all that interested in helping someone she has just fucked find his girlfriend. Lux gathers up his belongings, making sure that his treasures are in his plastic bag along with Pearl's reel of film.

Inside the small Liberation Computers office Pearl is drunk on brandy and Nicky is sitting staring at the wall and Mike is still trying to be extra pleasant to Marcus.

"Have some brandy. A cup of tea? That's a good game you're mak-ing, I could never make one that good, yep, you certainly are a genius when it comes to making computer games, I wish I had your skill, are you sure you wouldn't like some brandy?"

Marcus stands up.

"Mike. I am sick of you being nice to me. At a rough guess I would say you had some bad experience at the hands of some blacks."

"Yes," screams Mike. "But it doesn't make me think any the worse of you! How did you know?"

"Because any time something like this happens you spend hours feeling guilty in case you are thinking some politically bad thoughts and try and make up for it by being extra nice to me. What happened?"

Mike hangs his head.

"I was singled out from a crowd and mugged."

"Wow." says Marcus. "What a surprise. And now, having a sneaking, tiny, minute feeling at the back of your head that just maybe the racists are right because you have been mugged, you are unable to cope."

Lord Yasmin's team stays level with Lux all through the final encounter. Perfumes from all around the world are brought in, aromas so obscure that none but the finest perfume-guessers in Japan could hope to name them.

When the last porcelain bowl arrives the watching crowd is deathly silent.

"Well?" enquires the judge, after a while.

Sweating with mental exertion, Yasmin's man opens his mouth.

"Quatrino, from Indonesia," he says.

"Wrong," says the judge, dramatically. "Chang Kwai Lux?"

Lux looks over at Yasmin. Yasmin edges out a piece of parchment with Lux's poem on it, threateningly. The poet ignores the threat.

"Gujidana, from the unmapped lands of the Western Red Men," pronounces Lux. "Much used, I believe, as a natural skin toner and moisturiser."

"Correct," says the judge.

Lux has won. The audience applaud wildly, in a polite restrained sort of way.

I absolutely can't stand any more of this, thinks Kalia, working her way weakly through Brixton. I will lose my mind if I am reincarnated on this Earth again. I used to be able to ignore much of the stupidity, ignorance, brutality, prejudice, exploitation, violence, evil, and everything else. Now I have to watch it every day on television. And then there's the adverts as well.

I will do anything to reach my total and return to the heavenly palace. Where has this heavenly descendant got to?

To much ceremonial flag waving, Lux has led his team to triumphant victory. Never again will the neighbouring hamlet be able to sneer at them.

Lord Yamamoto personally congratulates him. Shimono throws her arms around him. Loved, the centre of attention, Lux is blissfully happy.

Yasmin concedes defeat politely before taking Lord Yamamoto aside for a quiet word.

Kalia, released from her room to join in the general celebration, wrestles her way in between Lux and Shimono.

"Leave now," she hisses. "There is going to be trouble."

"What trouble?" says Lux. "I am the hero of the hour. Have some sake."

Back in Liberation Computers, Marcus continues lecturing the guilty Mike.

"No doubt at this very minute a thousand racist acts are being committed by whites against blacks which will all go totally unreported anywhere. You, however, somehow expecting blacks to be perfect so as to fit in with your politics, cannot cope with a racist attack yourself. Kindly take your guilt feelings somewhere else and leave me to finish my Nicaragua computer game."

There is an awkward silence.

Lord Yamamoto thunders back into the room and has it cleared by his bodyguards.

"Is this true?" he demands, brandishing Lux's romantic poems.

"Yes," beams Lux. "You don't mind, do you? Everyone knows the Emperor's nephew is a moron, it would be a tragedy to marry Shimono off to him. They wouldn't have a thing to talk about."

Lux is taken outside. There is a brief ceremony before he is beheaded with the family sword which is kept sharp specially for this sort of occasion.

Idiot, thinks Kalia later, supervising his funeral. You just have no idea, do you?

"Come on," says Lux, walking up the road with Sebastian. "I'll show you where the Enterprise Centre is. Don't worry, the riot isn't so bad now."

"Is it always like this?" asks Sebastian, ashen-faced, clambering over some burnt-out rubbish bins.

"I don't think so," replies Lux. "Though I don't generally take much notice. I'm always too busy writing poetry and looking for Pearl."

I don't believe this, thinks Sebastian. I'm an accountant. I'm not the sort of person who has to cope with inner-city disturbances. He is rapidly going off the idea of sorting out a trouble spot for Coca Cola. He will ask them to send him somewhere quiet.

And nor am I the sort of person who keeps plunging into homoerotic fantasies of past lives, he continues, the filthy streets in front of him alternating with guilt-inducing thoughts of Lux and longing for Maybeline.

"Are you a crooked accountant?" asks Lux, making conversation.

"Certainly not."

"You want some blues? I pocketed a few."

"No."

"They'll give you energy."

"I don't take drugs."

"What do you do?"

"I'm an accountant."

"What for?"

"What do you mean what for?"

"What are you an accountant for?"

"I'm not an accountant for anything."

"What do accountants do?"

"Accounts."

"What accounts?"

"Business accounts."

"What for?"

Sebastian clutches his head. He is having erotic fantasies about an imbecile.

Johnny stumbles into view. "There he is," he screams, pointing at Lux. "Get him."

Lux, not knowing what Johnny is wanting but not willing to find out, heads for a wall, full speed.

"I will kill Lux," snarls Grub, crammed in a crowded police cell.

"Ha!" snorts Eugene. "Big talk. You are full of big talk."

"Shut up."

"Shut up yourself. And next time you want to burn down a tree try doing it when there isn't a van-load of policemen about. You must be the thickest person I know."

"Oh yeah?" retorts Grub. "Well who was it got a first in astrophysics from Cambridge? You or me?"

21

LUX, NOT REALISING that Johnny is after the genetic programme in his carrier bag, assumes he is just some madman, unless he is a poetry critic.

Lux knows that his poetry is too modern for some people's taste. His radical version of "I wandered lonely as a cloud" suffered terrible criticism one night from an intellectual friend of Mike's who claimed it was not possible that Wordsworth was feeling guilty about murdering babies when he wrote it.

"How do you know he never murdered any babies?" demanded Lux. "The daffodils could well be child substitutes."

"Well if he did it never made it into any biography I've read."

"It could have been hushed up. Any close reading of Wordsworth reveals him to be a total psychopath. He must have been guilty about something. Why else did he keep wandering around in fields? I suspect he was a cannibal."

Jumping down from the wall jars Lux and makes him reel. The drugs speed up his metabolism and speed up his mind and he is gripped with a terrible passion to find Pearl and give her the film and make everything all right.

But blood loss from his head wound along with huge drug abuse is starting to take its toll. Even Lux's healthy system cannot entirely cope and he starts to stumble along.

Some passersby, heading home as the riot quietens, help him to his feet. He clutches determinedly onto his carrier bag and walks on but trips over a chewing-gum machine, unfilled for years but left in place on the street till knocked over by a surging mob.

An ambulance pulls up.

"Looks like we reached you just in time," says the friendly ambulance driver and bundles him into the back.

"No," wails Lux, desperate not to be taken away to hospital when Pearl needs him, but his protests are useless and they start driving off, lights flashing.

"I'm perfectly healthy, I must find Pearl before the computer police get to her," he says, and starts to struggle.

"Drive fast," shouts the attendant to the driver. "His mind is starting to go."

"My mind is not starting to go," protests Lux. "I'm perfectly alright. Listen, I'll prove it." He launches into a poem, to his mind a very sane thing to do.

"'Where is your fabled Doric beauty?
The fringe of your towers, Corinth, your ancient properties,
The temples of Gods and men's homes,
The women of the city of Sisyphus . . .'

"See? I'm fine. Would you like to hear the next verse?" The attendant starts holding him down and mopping his head with a damp cloth.

"Stop for nothing," he yells at the driver. "This is serious."

Some people from the street outside enter the Enterprise Centre, push past the doorman and wander around looking for some way to carry on the excitement of the night.

Everywhere is locked except Liberation Computers, which they enter. There they intimidate Mike, Marcus, Nicky and Pearl, smiling at them, walking around pushing buttons on the computers, taking some brandy, sitting down beside the two women, talking about the violence they have done tonight, fingering pockets that may contain knives.

Intimidating other people is a good way to carry on your excitement.

Kalia meets Sebastian again. The meeting causes her more nausea and headache although she still does not realise that it is Sebastian's doing.

The accountant is reeling up the street.

She doesn't really like him, but supposes she should help. After all, the birds did say he was heading for serious trouble. And helping him then might be her ticket back into Heaven.

Lux resigns himself to being taken to hospital. When he arrives he will just have to slip out of a side exit and walk back to Brixton.

Normally he might be pleased at the opportunity of lying around in hospital for a while with hordes of doctors and nurses all looking after him while he lies in bed eating grapes and writing poetry. In fact he imagines it would be quite a nice life with no people from the social security dropping hints that he should try getting a job and maybe the whole ward full of patients flocking round to listen to his poems and nurses being nice to him and helping him fix his hair but of course at this moment he has more important things to do.

The ambulance comes to a halt.

"Are we there?"

Stones start to crash around the sides of the vehicle. Unable to pass an overturned car, it is a sitting target.

"The animals," says the attendant, temporarily releasing his grip on Lux. "Have they no respect for the medical profession?"

What a stroke of luck, thinks Lux, and waits for his chance.

There is a knock on the door and the helmeted and visored face of a policeman appears.

"You can't get through this way," he says, his riot shield protecting him from the hail of rocks. "You'll have to go back."

"But we have a very sick patient in here."

"I'm feeling much better now," says Lux, sprinting for freedom.

"Damn," says the ambulanceman. "I never saw anyone escape from an ambulance before. That's the second one tonight."

"He doesn't look very sick to me," comments the policeman, looking at Lux's quickly departing figure.

He gets back on the job, not having time to stand around chatting with medical crews. He has a riot to control and later he will have to make out a report on the desperate criminals he arrested earlier in the evening for burning down a tree, just one of many senseless acts of vandalism he has witnessed that night.

Inside Liberation Computers it is tense. Mike tries to defuse the situation by being friendly.

"We are a socialist computer cooperative," he says weakly, as one of the invaders pockets some electrical leads and picks up a keyboard, looking as if he may steal it as well. Mike is disturbed. He feels that a socialist computer cooperative should not be suffering at the hands of rioters.

"Yes," continues Marcus. "Good riot."

The gang carry on pocketing things, not very interested that Liberation Computers thought it was a good riot.

"Are you queer?" demands one of them, aggressively, noticing Mike's Gay Pride badge.

"What the fuck do you think you're doing?" demands Pearl, standing up, as someone touches her.

Lux, excited and triumphant, scrambles his way back into Brixton by way of the rows of gardens in the side streets, arriving finally at the centre, where assorted newsmen are now drinking tea in plastic cups, including one newsman who has a cut face with blood matted down his cheek but is still sticking to his task.

"Hello," says Lux, brandishing the can containing Pearl's film. "I am Lux, a big filmmaker. I've just been out in the thick of it, the rioters attacked my camera crew and killed them all but I managed to fight them off and save this roll of film, probably it will win me a prize when the next journalists' award ceremony rolls around. Apart from the scenes of carnage, the most interesting thing I filmed was Lux the Poet, a young genius who lives in these parts."

"Lux the filmmaker and Lux the Poet?"

"Many talented people are called Lux. This one was thrilling the rioters with a series of liberation poems. What have you all been doing? Hanging round here in safety? It's no good hiding, you know, you have to get out where the action is if you want to be a success in this business."

Everyone stares. Lux by this time is no longer the perfectly made-up creature who set out earlier in the evening. The jagged forest of his hair is now mangled around his head, with blood, setting gel, soap, sugar, hairspray, squirrel fur, and some assorted riot debris all oozing out to dribble down his neck and collar. His coat, a shabby affair at the best of times, is ripped in three places and his left foot is sticking out of his baseball boot. Most of his skin is filthy from the smoke and the crawling round in gardens, and those bits of his face that aren't dirty are smeared with cocaine, lipstick, and mascara. The general effect is something like Lana Turner through a mincing machine.

Lux, not realising there is anything unusual about his appearance, thinks he has an attentive audience and is about to launch into a poem or continue his story when something diverts his attention. There is a scent in the air he recognises. The air is still thick with smoke but Lux knows he can distinguish something.

Of course. It is the distinctive smell of Pearl's organic moisturiser. Bought from the local health-food store, it smells like nothing else.

She is somewhere close. His eyes blaze with happiness and he pushes his way through the reporters.

"There is the Enterprise Centre."

Kalia points.

"Thank you," says Sebastian. "You have been very helpful. Tonight has been terrible. I've been chased around by rioters and harangued by an imbecile with red and yellow hair. This place is disgusting. Everyone here makes me sick."

He leaves and Kalia wanders on, not knowing any more what she is meant to be doing.

Lying with a Friend under a Burnt-out Truck

"I'm cold," says Lux, shivering.

22

THE JANE AUSTEN MERCENARIES spend the night and part of the next morning in police cells before being released without any charges being made because there is so much confusion and so many charges to be laid against other people that they are not worth bothering about. But with no demo tape to play the record producer, they never do get to make the record.

"Kalia!" Lux shouts across the street, and hurries across, smiling wildly.

"What've you been doing? I've been talking to a squirrel and jumping out of burning trees and being filmed by TV cameras then I got forced into bed by a girl called Jean and I helped out this strange accountant then I got kidnapped by an ambulance and driven for miles so I had to break free and make a run for it before they did an operation on me or something then I crawled through gardens for miles till I picked up Pearl's scent and now I'm gonna take her the film then I saw you across the street."

"Lux, you are a terrible liar."

"It's all true. How about you? What've you been doing?"

"Oh, walking around, helping people. What were you doing to that accountant?"

"Nothing. I was friendly."

"Well he certainly doesn't like you."

"I expect he is wrapped up in guilt feelings because he is madly attracted to me. It happens all the time."

"How do you know he is madly attracted to you?"

"I can always tell. No doubt he has a girlfriend somewhere who wouldn't approve. I didn't really like him."

"Neither did I. As a descendant of Heaven he is a big disappointment."

"It was him?"

"Yes."

"Oh. He seemed a little strange. How did he manage as King of Sparta?"

"Fairly well, in the end."

Pearl picks up the phone.

"Security?" she says. "Get up to Liberation Computers and help us out. We're being harassed by a mob."

"Hey, bitch, what did you do that for?"

There is a pause while the gang contemplate some violence against Pearl, who stands protectively in front of Nicky.

Two security men arrive.

"We've called the police," they say. "They're downstairs now." The gang leave.

Afterwards Mike tells Pearl he doesn't think she should have done that because he does not really approve of calling the police on people and maybe getting them arrested, and Pearl says this is fine in theory but what else are you meant to do when someone is harassing you or about to attack you, and Mike has to agree that it is a difficult problem. And he finds the fact that some people in a riot against oppression were quite happy to oppress him for being gay another difficult problem.

Lux, still unaware of Pearl's exact whereabouts but knowing she is close, is stopped only yards away by a police cordon. He and Kalia are forced to turn back.

"Don't worry," says Kalia. "We'll work our way round."

"The street was closing, the city was closing, would we be the lucky ones to make it?" mumbles Lux.

A van draws up.

"Want a lift?" says the driver, a woman in overalls. On the side of the van it says Stockwell Women's Lift Service.

"We are out looking for people in trouble," says a woman in the back to them, as the van drives off.

"Thank you," says Lux. "Drop us near the Enterprise Centre."

"One moment," says the woman. "Are you female?"

"Not exactly," replies Lux. "Although I do get a lot of harassment from men on scaffolding."

The van draws to a halt and Lux is bundled out.

"Don't expect a big contribution from me when my royalties start pouring in," bawls Lux as it drives away.

"You should have told them you were having a sex change," says Kalia, who has loyally left the van with him.

"I never thought of that. Oh well. Let's keep looking."

Sebastian never makes it to his rendezvous. He is spotted by Johnny and arrested on suspicion of stealing the genetic programme.

Kalia and Lux, approaching, see it happen.

"Aren't you going to help?" whispers Lux, hiding round a corner so as Johnny doesn't see him.

"No."

"But he's the descendant of Heaven. It might be the important good deed that gets you back."

"I don't care. I'm sick of it. I don't want to help people I don't like any more. If a famous mythological figure turns up in this century as a power hungry accountant who harasses his secretaries he isn't going to get any assistance from me."

"How do you know he harasses his secretaries?"

"My powers are returning."

They walk on.

"Did I ever meet Helen of Troy?"

"Fortunately, no."

"Did I ever settle down happily with anyone?"

"Yes," lies Kalia.

"Do you think Pearl will fall in love with me?"

"Yes," says Kalia, lying again.

She is sad. She is beginning to think that she will never reach her total.

Happy Science has to abandon the genetic programme. Dr. Carlson retires a twisted and broken man, spending the rest of his life rambling about how he was unfairly denied a Nobel Prize.

The company stays successful, however, led by Mr. Socrates into new profitable areas of fast food research and better video cassettes.

"Hello Gerry," says Lux, as they meet. "What are you doing still wandering around?"

"Nothing much. I've lost a manuscript."

"Have this one," says Lux kindly.

"Where did you get this?" screams Gerry, recognising it as Mary Luxembourg's.

"I can't remember. Is it important? I'm looking for Pearl. I know she's close."

"She's in the Enterprise Centre."

"Brilliant," says Lux. "Did she mention me? Did she imply she was falling in love with me?"

"No."

"Did she mention anything about wanting to fuck me?"

"You disgust me," says Gerry. "There is more to relationships than having sex."

"We've been through all the other bits. We've been through sex as well. But I'm still enthusiastic."

Gerry gives him a look of contempt but the three of them head for the Enterprise Centre together.

"Look," says Lux, "a fox."

They watch as a fox runs out of some bins and along an alleyway, then they witness one of the most violent sights that any of them sees the entire night: a last battle by some particularly determined rioters with some police who have been tracking them over the rooftops with the aid of the helicopter spotlight. Determined not to be arrested, two men and a woman clamber down a drainpipe and make a run for it.

Two policemen set their dogs after them. The dogs run, jaws open, vicious and angered by the noise and confusion of the night.

"Here doggies," says Lux.

The dogs stop to lick his face.

"What's the idea?" demand the policemen.

"I can't help it. Animals love me."

He pats them on the head.

The three making the getaway have no chance. Despite Lux diverting the dogs, they are surrounded but, unusually determined, they fight furiously so that more and more policemen have to pile in and it becomes a bloody and one-sided mêlée of boots and truncheons and hate-filled yells.

"Stop hitting them," says Gerry, but no one takes any notice.

The bodies are carried away face down.

"Pigs," snorts Gerry. "They are disgusting."

"Fancy seeing a fox here," says Lux. "It is good the way they are starting to live in cities. What happened next in the perfume contest, Kalia?"

Sebastian is led off as a suspect in the Happy Science scandal. He is later cleared of complicity in the affair, but, missing his rendezvous with Ace Headhunters, does not make it to a position of wealth in Coca Cola. Maybeline is not impressed.

However, he is still a sought-after person, and may yet end up as something important.

But it will take him a very long time to get over the sight of the naked Lux.

Before Kalia has to face telling Lux that what happened next in the perfume-guessing contest was that he was beheaded, Lux grabs her arm.

"There's that man again. The one that arrested the accountant. He's after me as well."

"Why?"

"I don't know. Some spurious reason, I expect. Unless he wants my autograph. No doubt I could put him off with some well-constructed story but I'm anxious to reach Pearl and give her the film."

Kalia is starting to feel better now that Sebastian is out of the area and no longer broadcasting psychic disturbance.

"You carry on," she says. "I'll divert him. That man is head of the computer police. But he is also Yasmin, and totally evil. You might find it hard to put him off."

Patrick, watching a specially extended late-night news bulletin, sees Lux approaching the Enterprise Centre, where, by coincidence, he meets Mike, out for another breath of fresh air.

"I don't believe it!" explodes Patrick, worst suspicions confirmed. "They've arranged a secret meeting in the middle of the riot!"

I'm not standing for this, he thinks, and puts on his coat.

Lux and Gerry enter the building. Gerry goes to use the phone while Lux rushes upstairs.

Too excited to control himself, he bursts into Liberation Computers and throws himself into Pearl's lap. Drunk, she overbalances and they collapse in a struggling heap onto the floor.

"Hello Pearl," he bawls, "I've saved your film."

Pearl is elated at getting her film back. She kisses Lux. Lux is elated at this and happiness prevails.

Kalia stands in front of Yasmin.

"Hello again," he says. "I have been having a very entertaining night. I love all troubles. I love to see people squirm. And I love to keep you here on Earth.

"You can't keep me here on Earth."

"Can't I? I know you hoped to save the heavenly descendant, Menelaus, King of Sparta, reborn as a power-hungry accountant. Well I have had him thrown in jail. So much for your good deeds."

"There will be plenty more opportunities."

"None that I cannot prevent."

Kalia bites her lip.

Yasmin grins, knowing he is getting to her.

"Later tonight I am going to arrest the small one with red and yellow hair. The effeminate one. I know you like him. I will also have his friends arrested. They are all implicated in robbing Happy Science."

"I'll prevent you."

"I doubt it. And if you did, would it count as an act of kindness? To you, yes, but to Heaven? Probably not."

"And," he adds maliciously, "even if it did count it wouldn't help you. You can't get back into Heaven. No one is keeping track of your good deeds any more. My master saw to that. You passed one million long ago. You are never going back."

"A woman made this film
  against
  the law
  of gravity," says Lux, on the floor in a heap with Pearl and the can
of film.
  "What?" says Pearl.
  "A poem by Adrienne Rich. And very appropriate. I love you."
  The general happiness is interrupted by Nicky bursting into tears.
  No one can cheer her up. Pearl tries being supportive and Lux gets
in the way and Marcus has to stop programming his computer game.
  "Can nobody help?"
  "It's a difficult case," says Mike, sagely. "Deep trauma from killing
her computer. She may never recover."
  "Surely there must be some cure?"
  "Not much research has been done on it yet. It's a comparatively
new disease."
  Pearl puts her arm round Nicky, though she still grasps her film
tightly and allows Lux to hold her arm, or the only bit of her arm he
can get hold of.
  "When I was young," says Lux, "I suffered a similar sort of thing
when my pet dog fell under the lawnmower. We had a terible time with
lawnmowers in my family. Anyway I was distraught but as soon as I got
a new puppy I felt much better."
  "So?"
  "So give Nicky a new computer. It is bound to help. I was a new
person when I got my new puppy. It completely restored me, while I
still had it."
  "What happened to it?"
  "It got eaten by an alligator when I took it to the zoo. I was never
very lucky with my pets. Still, a new computer substitute is bound to
help."
  Lux is being cunning as well as helpful, thinking that possibly if
Nicky is wrapped up in a new computer then Pearl will have more time
for him.

Mike goes and drags something out of a cupboard.

"Here," he says to Nicky. "Take this. It's a new model we haven't started to use yet."

Nicky takes the computer and looks at it. She smiles.

"Lux saves the day again," says Lux. "Thwarting the Jane Austen Mercenaries, saving Pearl's film, solving Nicky's problems, talking to TV cameras, guarding squirrels, saving rioters from police dogs . . ."

"You didn't save them," says Gerry, fresh from reporting to *Uptown* that both Mary Luxembourg and the riot are fine.

"Saving rioters from police dogs," continues Lux, ignoring the interruption, "escaping from ambulances, leaping from burning trees, writing poems, there seems to be nothing I can't do. Good prevails all round."

"No it doesn't," protests Gerry. "Outside there is the remains of a riot and the whole area is totally depressed. I don't see you doing any good in that direction."

Lux goes to the window.

"The riot was all my fault," he yells. "I started it. I am responsible. Now everyone stop rioting and go home." He pauses. "Which direction is the Houses of Parliament?"

"Over there."

Lux points his head in the vague direction of Parliament. "Give everybody a job and make things better! Pump money into the local economy. Do I make myself clear?"

He leaves the window. "There. I've done my best. Would anyone like to hear a poem I made up while I was hiding up the tree?"

No one volunteers to listen to the poem.

"Stop ignoring me," says Nicky to Pearl.

"What?"

"Stop ignoring me. Since Lux brought the film back you've been hugging it like I don't exist."

Pearl is a little exasperated.

"Well you're too busy with your new computer to pay me any attention. All night I've been keeping you safe and all you're grateful for is a new computer."

"Well no wonder I need a computer when you're always too busy with your film to pay me any attention. All you've done for months is to make that damn film."

Slightly drunk, the two women argue.

Ha, thinks Lux, pleased. The new computer plan was a masterstroke. Soon they'll never speak to each other again.

Suddenly catching sight of his reflection in the window, he realises what a shambles he is. He has temporarily forgotten his vanity in the excitement of meeting Pearl. Figuring that he ought to make himself look nice for her he goes to hunt for a toilet to make himself look presentable.

In the corridor he meets Kalia.

"Hi Kalia," he says cheerfully. "Pearl and Nicky are having a terrible argument. Soon they'll never speak to each other again. Pearl is bound to fall in love with me."

He stops.

"What's wrong?" he asks, finally noticing that she is looking immensely sad.

Kalia tells him about her never getting back into Heaven.

So that is where they got to, thinks Johnny, passing by outside with his computer police squad, and hearing Lux's voice.

"Listen," says Kalia, entering Liberation Computers. "Johnny and his squad of computer police are still hunting for you." Her powers of foreknowledge are returning, and despite her own problems she wishes to be helpful. "I think they will be here soon."

"What'll we do?" says Pearl. "They're after Nicky and me. We'd better run."

"Too late," says Kalia. "I can feel them coming. Lock the door and keep silent. We'll hide till we can think of something better."

Outside it is now quiet. The police are in control and will continue
to patrol the streets in numbers for months to come. Round corners
they will sit in rows in their green buses, waiting for trouble.

There will be an inquiry into the riot, like there was an inquiry into
the last one.

Newspapers will condemn it as violent hooliganism, and call for
wider police powers. They may mention that both blacks and whites
were involved, but will be sure to put a picture on the front page of a
young black throwing a petrol bomb. They will give a cursory mention
to the bad conditions in the area.

Uptown will support it as a justified action against oppression. They
will give a cursory mention to all the poor people who got robbed and
the women who got raped.

The government will announce a new programme for helping the
inner cities. The new pink pavement will be cleaned up and the job
centre will get a facelift.

Johnny prowls the corridors with his four men. To an outsider the building is a little confusing with small rooms and corridors everywhere, and
they spend a long time searching without finding anything.

"Perhaps they're not here," suggests one of his men. They are all
tired and want to go home.

Johnny considers it. They have been all over the building and found
no trace. Perhaps they should abandon the hunt for the night. After all,
they have already arrested one major conspirator.

For a brief second it seems that Liberation Computers may
escape.

Patrick appears. He has come to give Mike a piece of his mind
about the secret meeting with Lux.

"Security," says Yasmin. "Do you mind stating your business?"

"I'm just calling in to Liberation Computers on the next floor," says
Patrick.

Everyone at Liberation Computers is becoming drunk as more emergency brandy is passed around.

"He saved my film," says Pearl to Kalia. "He told me all about leaping into the blazing inferno. I guess he is not so useless."

Kalia is looking thoughtful.

"Right, Mike," shouts Patrick, unlocking the door and bursting in. "What's the idea of walking out on me and then carrying on with floozies in the street? And what about the secret rendezvous with Lux? Don't deny it, I saw it on television."

"You're all under arrest," says Johnny, appearing behind him, "for complicity in the theft of a secret genetic programme. And wrecking Happy Science property, stealing the programme, and interfering with legitimate police business. And I will have to confiscate this film which contains classified material from Happy Science, illegally gained."

In the toilet, Lux, fixing his make-up, is thoughtful. He is thinking about Kalia and thinking about everything else.

Pearl, film threatened, tries to hit Johnny with the brandy bottle but he blocks the blow and a fight ensues, a fight in which Pearl and the rest have little chance and Liberation Computers suffers more damage.

"Excuse me," says Lux very loudly, reappearing in the room, face shining. The fight stops.

"I am aware that you do not take me or my poetry seriously. Nevertheless, I am now going to read a poem. I have just written it. It is about my friend Kalia, and me. It's called 'On being exiled from Heaven for three thousand years, on being exiled from Pearl for ever.'"

He pulls out a sheet of paper from his carrier bag.

Outside in the blackness of the night firemen dampen down some remaining flames and the newsmen go home to bed.

Lux's poem is heart-rendingly beautiful. It talks of Kalia's misery in eternal exile and Lux's misery in eternal loneliness. Everyone in the room forgets everything else and listens.

Lux, so eager to write the poem that he didn't finish his eye make-up, reads it out, a steady voice in the silence.

His voice sucks in the onlookers. The poem makes their hearts ache. Every sad and lonely feeling ever felt between Heaven and Earth haunts each line, every hopeless defeat ever suffered by humanity is contained in its words.

He finishes. People are wiping away tears.

Yasmin sniffs loudly before turning abruptly and leaving.

Confused, his men follow.

23

IN THE SILENCE of Yasmin's departure, nobody speaks.

Lux, having finally had a dramatic effect on the real world, is a little embarrassed, and stares at his feet.

Kalia slips out quietly.

Pearl and Nicky sit holding hands and staring into each other's eyes while Mike and Patrick huddle in a corner, all relationships reconciled after listening to the poem.

Liberation Computers is a wreck after the fight. Another failure for the social security's start-your-own-business scheme. Marcus starts tidying up.

Outside Kalia meets Yasmin.

He tells her that Lux's poem has made him cry for the first time in three thousand years. He is going to abandon his persecution of Kalia and inform the proper authorities in Heaven that her sentence is completed.

He leaves. His men, not understanding, hang around. Kalia, unsure whether to believe him or not, wanders back inside. There is little of the riot left anywhere.

Suddenly her ability to read the future returns in full and she starts running up the stairs.

With Marcus busy clearing up, Mike and Patrick in a corner, and Pearl, Nicky, Pearl's film, and the new computer in a close embrace, there is no one for Lux to talk to. For the first time in his life he feels awkward.

"Well," he says. "I'm going to look for a TV camera."

"Lux," says Pearl.

"What?"

"Nothing."

Lux crosses to the window and peers out.

"A film crew," he says, excited, returning somewhat to his normal state. "There's a film crew out there. They're filming the mopping-up operations. Hey! Look up here! It's me, Lux the Poet!"

He leans out of the window and starts shouting out some of his favourite lines.

"Be careful Lux," says Pearl, seeing that he is a little unsteady. "You're not well."

"Of course I'm well," says Lux. "I'm an important local poet. How well can you get?"

He climbs onto the window sill, waves to the camera, faints from loss of blood, and falls to the ground outside.

Gerry is on his way back to personally deliver his riot report to the all-night emergency editorial meeting at the offices of *Uptown*.

When he arrives he finds Mary Luxembourg sitting in.

"Hi," he says. "I've brought your manuscript."

"What's this I hear about a retrospective?"

"What retrospective? Nothing to do with me."

Pearl rushes downstairs, barges past Kalia, and runs out into the street in time to see Lux picking himself up off the pavement.

"Lux, you idiot. You trying to kill yourself?"

It seems miraculous that he is unhurt. But, stunned by the fall, Lux no longer quite realises what is happening. Seeing the remains of the computer police in the distance, Johnny's men now standing leaderless, he thinks that Pearl is still in danger. He grabs her arm and runs. Pearl runs with him.

Round a corner he dives under a burnt-out truck.

"We'll hide here for a while," he says.

Sebastian is released from the police station, freed pending further investigation. The Jane Austen Mercenaries walk out at the same time, silently depressed.

Sebastian phones Maybeline, but she isn't home.

"What the hell is this?" demands Mary Luxembourg, brandishing her novel, the only copy of which is now covered in Lux's poems, scrawls, and alterations.

"Your novel," replies Gerry. Not actually having read it, he doesn't realise there is anything wrong with it.

"Don't count on any endorsements from me," says the author, a little upset.

"It wasn't such a bad night," says Lux under the truck. "I get stuffed full of cocaine, I write a good poem, I meet a nice woman from Scotland and a nice woman from Heaven. And I end up lying under a truck with you, which is best. We can leave when the riot finishes."

"The riot is finished."

"Can't be," says Lux. "I can still hear all the shouting."

"That was a good poem," says Pearl.

"Thank you." Lux shivers and pulls his coat tighter around him.

"I'm pleased you're getting on well with Nicky," he says.

Blood loss and huge internal injuries from the fall get the better of him. He coughs, sighs, and dies.

"Lux?" says Pearl. "Lux?"

She twists her head round and stares into the small dark space beneath the truck, expecting him at any minute to sit up and start quoting *Paradise Lost*, just to prove he knows it. Lux, however, is too dead to quote any more poetry.

Kalia appears with Nicky, and helps Pearl out from under the vehicle.

"You go home," she says. "I'll wait here for an ambulance."

The night is busy with patrolling policemen but still and quiet in Kalia's soul.

Waiting for the ambulance she has the sudden conviction that a good turn she can do for Lux will be the one that gets her back into Heaven. So she cleans his face and arranges his hair a little, knowing he would like to look his best.

Nothing happens. She is not returned to Heaven.

The ambulance arrives and takes Lux away and Kalia walks off into the night.

"Goodbye Lux," she says, without emotion. "You never managed to fit in anywhere, did you?"

Round the corner she comes across a tramp, shivering because someone has stolen his coat.

Kalia takes off her own coat and gives it to him. She tingles slightly, and de-materialises, saved from any more suffering on Earth.

An Afterword
as written on martin-millar.blogspot.com

Tuesday, December 9th, 2008

MORE OF MY BACKLIST UNLEASHED ON THE WORLD

The Millar backlist assault on the world continues. I just received the manuscript for the re-issue of *Lux the Poet*, which will be reprinted some time next year. And only yesterday the postman brought me a box of copies of *Milk, Sulphate, and Alby Starvation* from the American publisher Soft Skull. This seems to be available on amazon.com already, although it hasn't reached amazon.co.uk yet.

Hmm. Can anyone actually prove I wrote all these books? I could deny it.

A brief story about when I was writing *Lux the Poet*: I was living in a small council flat in Brixton. I shared the flat with a primary school teacher who I liked, but was rarely there, and a young man who was a serious alcoholic, as was his boyfriend. They were continually drunk, probably too drunk to have sex, but they were both fond of spanking. Being so drunk, they weren't concerned about privacy, and used to perform, or attempt to perform, spanking sessions in the living room.

Meanwhile I stayed in my own room, writing *Lux the Poet* on an old word-processor. So I could hear the spanking, which would have been strange enough anyway, but because of their extreme drunkenness and lack of coordination, it happened at an unbelievably slow rate. I'd write one sentence of *Lux*, and hear a vague slapping noise. And then I'd write a bit more, and after a few more sentences, there'd be another spanking noise, followed by some loud struggling as they fell off the couch and scrambled around for their cans of special brew. And then, some time later, there'd be another vague slapping sound. Really, you wouldn't believe that any spanking could possibly be carried on in such a slow and disorganised fashion. Sometimes they'd actually miss the target, which you'd think would be practically impossible. Hours later I'd find them collapsed, semi-naked and unconscious on the living room floor. Both of them by this time quite emaciated young men, from alcohol abuse. I was pleased when I moved out of that flat.

If you're looking for some relaxing viewing—like for instance if you've just taken a rhubarb crumble out of the oven and you're planning it eat it while watching TV—then I recommend not watching "Happiness," Todd Solondz's grim black comedy from 1999. I found myself doing this a few nights ago, and it was definitely a poor choice. I've rarely seen so much uncomfortable heavy breathing and squirming onscreen, or such a cast of unlikeable characters. But it's a good film too, so I didn't want to stop watching it. It kind of spoiled my rhubarb crumble relaxation though. I hereby resolve never to watch anything serious ever again, and stick to watching Tokyo Mew Mew on Pop TV. Except now it's changed channels to Popgirl TV and I don't have that channel. Damn these schedulers. Fine, I'll watch it on YouTube instead.

Posted by Martin Millar